THE LAST TRAIN WEST

JEAN M. PRESTBROTEN

ISBN: 146990408X
ISBN 13: 9781469904085

This is the World War II survival story of a German woman, Margarete (Gretel) Sennhenn Prestbroten.

"Girlie, you don't know what it is like to have war on your soil," she told me. "For you Americans, war is always 'over there.' Not since your Civil War have you had battles right outside your door. When you see war the way I did, and you have lived amongst it, it is from a whole new perspective."

This, her survival story, is true in essence, and much of the material in this book I derived from some notes, a memoir of sort, that she wrote prior to her death in 1976. I used the memoir as an outline, and have fictionalized and expounded on what she revealed.

I hope you enjoy this story of WWII from a different point of view: that of a kindergarten teacher in occupied Poland.

I thank my husband for his support and for allowing me to tell his mother's true story in a fictional way.

CHAPTER 1

Gretel Sennhenn's hands trembled while holding the ominous-looking white envelope trimmed in black, a death notification. Suspecting the news was about her fiancé, she picked off the red-wax seal and then abruptly handed the envelope to her mother.

"*Ist es* Wilhelm, Mamma?"

"*Ja, lieb.*"

Gretel shuffled her way to a window in their fourth-story apartment that overlooked the bustling city of Kassel, Germany. Her legs were shaking so hard, she was glad when her mother grabbed a chair for her to sit on and a towel in case she threw up. The family had endured the deaths of so many family and friends since the beginning of World War II, the scene was almost redundant.

Gretel, now enveloped in sobs, managed to cry out, "Why the war, Mamma? Why did Wilhelm have to die in a field hospital bombing when he was just there to help? He was such a good doctor!" The question was rhetorical; Mamma gave no answer and none was expected.

Quickly and valiantly, Gretel regained control and stood up, silently staring out the window and compulsively twisting a strand of her chestnut-colored hair around her right forefinger, a habit she'd had since childhood. Marching music blared from the radio. Abruptly, the radio station signed off its broadcast with a perfunctory and thunderous, "Heil Hitler!" Gretel did a quick pivot, almost tripping on the Oriental rug, and looked up at her mother, who was a full six inches taller.

"Mamma," she said, "I am twenty-six years old. I cannot live with you and Father any longer. Wilhelm and I were to marry when the war was over. I was supposed to wait for him, but this will change everything. This war is three years old now. How many military must die at the West Front or elsewhere? How many citizens will sit *here* waiting to die? Well, not me!"

Gretel's mother, a rotund woman with salt-and-pepper hair, placed the envelope on top of an antique serving cart, took off her apron, and asked, "What will you do, Gretel?"

"I am a good kindergarten teacher. I have cared for children of all ages and taught them everything the Nazi Party says I must. I am the best! Headquarters said so! With the men at war and the bombings in the cities, mothers are heading to the country with their children. I do not want to stay here, where the kindergarten attendance is dropping."

"Where will you go?"

"I can request a transfer to occupied Poland. Many respite homes for German children are opening up there. The young ones are safer in Poland, being away from the bombing of the German cities that is, and I will be safer, too." Gretel patted her mother's hand, took a deep, ragged breath, and in nearly a whisper, said, "Tomorrow, Father and I need to talk about what needs to be done if…if we do not see each other again."

"Oh, *Gott*," Mamma said despondently.

"*Gott? Nein*! Hitler? *Ja*!" Gretel screamed.

The war had hardened Gretel to where she no longer believed in God, so she slammed the door, pulled up her socks, and scampered down the stairs into the chilly September night.

Gretel walked to the library building where she and the rest of the class of 1939 had received their degrees. What a class it was! As always, the instructors taught how to handle the physical, medical, emotional, and educational needs of German youth, but now Nazi theory was also an important part of the curriculum.

How proud Gretel had been when party leaders chose her to head one of the most difficult schools of all: a home for disadvantaged and delinquent teens and preteens whom social services sent so they might be made proper Hitler youth and their parents better citizens. She managed things so efficiently that those at party headquarters had been able to increase the group's size from fifteen to fifty-two. Now, in September 1942, only ten children remained in her care, so there was little for Gretel to do; that played a large part in her decision to go to Poland.

Her legs were trembling, so Gretel sat on the front steps of the building, recalling happier days at Kindergarten Teacher Seminary. It was for her a time that generated fond memories. She twisted a strand of her hair around her fingers and cried a cascade of tears over Wilhelm and the war in general.

A lone figure approached. It was a police officer.

"Are you well, miss?"

"Yes, I am."

He gave a minuscule tip of his hat and urged her not to linger on the streets at night. She wiped her face with a handkerchief, thanked him, and went home.

A week later, her transfer approved, Gretel prepared for the trip to Poland. She was to report to the National Social Welfare Organization office in Posen, the seat of the occupation government, where she would receive further orders. She spent four days getting official papers in order, banking, packing, and writing letters.

One of the letters was to her younger brother, Helmut, a member of the Nazi SS. It was generic in nature and unemotional, since he probably would not receive it. There had been no news of him for six months. His tall, blonde-haired, Aryan physique, much adored by the Hitler regime, was so different from short, dark-haired Gretel's, that she was admittedly jealous. She had often complained to her mother about being female, a nondescript female at that, in a world of male dominance.

Gretel's mother was inconsolable when it was time for her daughter to leave, and she would not relinquish her grip on her.

"Is my beautiful Helmut dead? Oh! Will you disappear too, dear?"

All Gretel could do in the end was push Mamma's hands away and promise to return. From the street, Gretel could see Mamma leaning over the window box, waving a handkerchief frantically, so she waved back at her and smiled.

* * *

"Father, I will not be gone long. You know that," Gretel said, when it came time to say their good-byes at the train station. "The super weapon is almost ready, and the war will be over soon."

She squinted into the sun to have one last look at her father, a tall man with thick, silver hair. Her mouth opened as if to say something, but no words would come. Without ceremony or a hug, she turned away. When her father called her name, Gretel bit her lip savagely. She managed only to whisper, "*Auf Wiedersehen.*"

Without another word, she buttoned her gray woolen coat snugly around her petite frame, picked up her suitcases, and plodded with them down the brick pathway. The train's engine was building up a full head of steam, and the sound of it muffled her whimpers.

The train trekked on toward Berlin. Despite the news that German troops had "pulled back to more favorable positions" and food rationing was in full swing, Gretel remained upbeat about the war. She could picture, in her mind's eye, the thousands of young people she had seen singing the national anthem in front of the Reichskanzlei. What a sight it had been! She could see as clearly as in the newsreels, Hitler himself promising the German people jobs and a good future! How proud she had been of their army on the day of the Blitzkrieg into Poland. How handsome were the soldiers! How magically that day had illuminated the German spirit! She could still hear the roar of the crowds shouting, "*Seig-Heil!*" She could smell the beautiful flowers the citizens placed near Hitler's ever-present picture on his birthday.

A scream of "*Bomben! Bomben!*" woke her from her daydreaming. The train screeched to a halt. It had reached Berlin, and the city was under attack. Sirens and people wailed. Planes roared. Passengers scrambled to get off the train and head for the air-raid shelter.

As Gretel was about to leave the train, a pale woman with a dirty green scarf and eyes like a pug puppy pleaded, "*Meine Kinde!*" then pushed her sleeping infant against Gretel's chest and motioned her to go. There was no time to ask her why she was so adamant about abandoning her child, so Gretel carried the baby one-handed by his corduroy breeches and presented her other hand to a burly trainman who helped her disembark. She ran as fast as her short legs could take her.

An hour and a half later, Gretel, the baby, and about eighty others were still in the air-raid shelter, huddled within its cold concrete walls. The child was squirming and protesting with high-pitched screams. Some already-weary individuals tired of it and began to complain. Gretel's eyes darted from person to person, her body language sending out visible pleas for help. Another woman, also with an infant, handed her child off to an elderly woman and approached Gretel.

"Hello, I am Clara. I have been watching you. He is not yours, is he? Give him to me."

To Gretel's speechless surprise, Clara began to nurse the little boy. Soon he was fast asleep, smelly diaper and all.

The train station was not the target of the attack, at least not this time. When the danger passed, Gretel found the baby's mother on the train, still sitting in the same seat. With a sigh of relief, Gretel gave the baby to her.

"A lady named Clara fed him. He's tired now."

"I cannot repay your kindness, or hers. Pardon me. My name is Birgit. It looks as if my son and I are both wet," she said, pointing to her chest. The two broke into giggles and several passengers turned to stare, looking much like a parliament of owls.

Gretel felt overheated and took off her coat, revealing a cranberry-colored, velvet-like jumper over an unusually expensive-looking white blouse.

"Pretty," Birgit said.

"Thanks. My name is Gretel. Look, Birgit, I think you owe me an explanation. Why wouldn't you come to the shelter? What were you thinking? You gave your child to a total stranger! Do you know what it was like for us in the shelter?"

"Do you know what it was like for me wondering how he was? I have a heart condition. I cannot run fast."

The words gave a solemn note to a rare moment of levity. Gretel settled back into the mohair-covered seat for a nap. She hadn't had a chance to find a restaurant while in Berlin and hunger pangs were setting in.

When the train arrived in Posen, Gretel was so anxious she blew small puffs of air through her lips to prevent hyperventilating. She retrieved a bundle of papers from her luggage, memorized the address of the National Social Welfare Organization, and fumbled through the paperwork to find the name of the person to whom she was to report. In her mind, she could hear her mother's oft-repeated words: "Remember to use only High German, Gretel! Stand erect, and stop playing with your hair!"

Gretel trudged along, suitcases in tow, and quickly found a shabby-looking but clean hotel. As at so many other places, posted on the door was a sign that read, "Germans only!" The clerk grudgingly placed Gretel's bags in her room, and then held out a pale, effeminate hand for a tip.

"Please tell me," she said, as she placed the coins in his palm. "Which direction is the National Social Welfare Organization office?"

"So, you work for the party?" he said. "Well, next time ask them to give you directions to it! It is six blocks north. By the way, if you want to stay any longer, you will have to pay each night in advance."

Gretel would waste no more conversation on what she felt was a perfect example of low-class Polish people. She was aware that Germans owned most of the businesses now. Surely, she told him, she would speak to the hotel proprietor when she returned.

"I will assume you are only tired and not deliberately rude," she said. "I thank you for the directions."

Gretel checked her watch and determined there would be no time to get something to eat. She ran all the way to the party office and entered the building sweaty and trembling. A stern-looking woman with rigid posture sat at a desk in the foyer. She checked Gretel's papers and pointed in the direction of a poorly lit hallway. Gretel smelled an unusual odor coming from the hallway, perhaps a cleaning solution.

Gretel pushed wide open the door to the room the woman directed her to and then stumbled over the threshold. Twenty other newcomers were in the party boss's waiting room, mostly nurses and teachers, like her. They sat quietly with their hands folded on their laps. Uneasiness crept in like a fog. Humiliated by her awkward entrance, Gretel avoided eye contact with anyone and lowered herself onto a wooden chair.

Without a greeting, the boss walked in and began to speak to the window: "You have come to work in an occupied country. You will tend to the German people only. I forbid you to assist any Pole, no matter what help he may need or what age he is. If he lies in a gutter, give him a kick and walk on. Now, as for the children: you will in no manner help the Polish misfits and miscarriages! We give their kind the same treatment they gave our own people in Danzig and Selica since the last war! In case you will ever forget my orders"—he turned to face them—"we have ways to make you remember! Good luck to you. Heil Hitler!"

The clack of his boot heels against the wood floor was the only sound she heard as he disappeared into his office.

Gretel had dealt with stern party bosses before, and she knew they did not have a genteel way about them, but this man had to be an aberration! All directives to German officials in Poland came from Berlin. Did they not know about this foul, ostentatious man? Someone should report him! Perhaps he was only teaching the newcomers to be aware and defensive in an occupied country with a hostile environment. But misfits? Miscarriages? The words made her knees weak.

As she swayed back and forth, she heard someone say, "Gretel! Are you sick?"

"*Nein. Ich bin hungrig.*"

When the dizziness subsided and she opened her eyes, Gretel at first thought she was hallucinating.

"*Ist es* Crystel?"

It was, indeed, her good friend Crystel! Crystel was the nurse who had taught most of her medical-related classes at the teachers' seminary! Had it really been two years ago already? In her rush to take her seat, Gretel had not noticed her. Crystel's hair looked dry now, and she had lost far too much weight, but Gretel could still see that sparkle in her eyes! Not even the stress of war or food rationing had changed that.

Crystel joined Gretel in search of a restaurant, and each ordered cabbage rolls with potatoes and tea. They made excited conversation and talked about the days at the kindergarten seminary, but neither mentioned the boss's speech.

While still sitting at the table, Crystel started rearranging the bobby pins in her prematurely gray hair. Gretel found this to be ill mannered, and rolled her eyes in disgust, but Crystel did not notice.

When she had finished primping, Crystel asked, "Whom do you see for assignment when we get to Konin tomorrow, Gretel?"

"Herr Klein."

"Me too. I guess most of us do."

"I want to make a good impression, Crystel. My future depends on it! If I do not get a decent assignment, I might be able to convince him otherwise. Have you heard anything about him?"

"No. Well, a little."

"So, what did you hear?"

"*Dieses schwein!* I hear he hates women and scratches his ass all day!"

"Crystel!" Gretel did not laugh. Instead, she assumed a haughty posture and spoke quietly through pursed lips. "I am hoping to get a good job here. Now be quiet. You'll ruin everything!"

"I am only teasing! I do not even know him."

Gretel pointed to a sign that read: "Silence! The enemy is listening!" These signs were everywhere: on trains, in restaurants, and in stores. As they indicated, it was not safe to mock or criticize the party, or any member of it. The nicely dressed gentleman next to you could be a party member or a spy.

"You know better than to say that, Crystel! Let's get out of here!" Gretel said.

"I am not finished eating."

"I could not care less! We are leaving."

A man at a counter stool spun around and stared at them. Had he heard what Crystel said? Perhaps he was only nosy because he heard the angry intonation in Gretel's voice. Gretel's heart pounded. He was looking directly at them. Worse, he was walking straight toward their table! She could scarcely breathe. Her hands were shaking. There were rumors of people disappearing after insulting the Nazis. They could not be true, could they?

Gretel displayed a forced smile. "My dear friend, it is time to leave. We have an early appointment in the morning." She kicked Crystel under the table, but the woman did not react. Her mouth was full and she simply kept chewing.

The man approached them and made a delicate hand gesture, subtly indicating Crystel should come with him. *This is it,* Gretel thought, *we are finished!*

"You ladies should be on your way," he said. "Posen is not a friendly city right now, and it is getting dark. I need to close up anyway. I do not stay open late anymore."

"Yes, I agree," said Crystel. "My friend was just mentioning that we ought to leave—weren't you, Gretel?" She pasted a smug grin on her face and patted Gretel's hand in a condescending manner. Gretel felt wilted.

"Oh! You are the owner?" she asked.

"Yes, obviously. Ladies? Are you ready?"

The women stepped outside and immediately heard the door lock behind them. Gretel jumped when she saw the shadow of someone exiting the side door of the restaurant. It was a young waiter carrying an armful of tablecloths and aprons. He was, apparently, on his way to the laundress. Another scare.

Gretel elbowed Crystel, "*Dumm Kopf!*"

That put Crystel on the defensive. "You haven't changed, Gretel! You are always so stiff and proper. For you, everything has to be in order, and you always play by the rules!"

"It is what makes me the best at my job! The party is very impressed with my work."

"I am good at my job, too, but you are just a party puppet! That is why they like you. You follow orders without question. I am eight years older than you are, and old enough to stop being naive like you are."

The words cut Gretel like a knife and so destroyed her ego that she hauled off and slapped Crystel.

She only had a short distance to run to the hotel. Even so, a pain in her side caused her to limp as she entered the building. An imaginary bell was ringing in her head. Its clapper banged out the words: "Party puppet! Naive! Party puppet! Naive!"

Gretel washed and dressed for bed, then opened the window to pour the contents of the chamber pot onto a weedy, fenced-in area, but it slipped from her hands. The impact when it hit the ground reduced it to shards. Could anything be worse? She lay in bed twisting her hair until it looked like frayed hemp rope. It wasn't until the early morning hours that she finally fell asleep, and even then, not for long. She had to pee again and there was no chamber pot. Reluctantly, she used the pitcher on the washstand.

The next morning Gretel's hunt for a café proved futile. Many stores and restaurants had been boarded up, their doors painted with a yellow Star of David. Gretel was not about to go to the restaurant that she and Crystel had eaten at the night before, so she sat on a park bench and threw pebbles at the pigeons. It seemed there was no food for them either.

A craggy-faced elderly lady wearing a gray jumper and a black babushka tottered toward her. She carried a beautiful woven basket draped with an exquisite, hand-embroidered linen cloth. This frail-looking Pole obviously came from a family that had once lived an elegant lifestyle, but today she sold rolls. Gretel hopped off the park bench and raised one finger. When the woman reached for the coin Gretel held, it became obvious that her arms were just bones with flesh hanging on them. Gretel gestured for another roll, and after she paid for it, gave it back. When she motioned for the woman to eat it, a toothless smile spread across her face as she nodded that she understood.

Gretel tossed a few crumbs from her roll onto the ground to the delight of the pigeons, but they scattered when a familiar voice shouted, "Gretel! Gretel Sennhenn!" It was Crystel at a dead run! "You have to come *now!* You have to come listen to the radio! Berlin is saying that Stalingrad will be ours. This war will be over soon. I know it!"

Gretel would not look Crystel in the eye; instead, she looked the opposite direction, focusing on a horse-drawn hearse.

"I will wait here, Crystel. I cannot be late for the train if I want to make a good impression on Herr Klein. Remember *him?*"

"Gretel, please, I am sorry if I insulted you, and I deserved to be slapped, but I will say this once: Listen to everything, but do not believe everything you hear. Trust your instincts, and do not question me any further. That is all I can say, Gretel. By the way, I see you have your bags with you. Why didn't you leave them at the hotel until the train is due?"

"I did not want to talk to anyone at the hotel, so I left early. That is all I can say."

The train to Konin was on time. The three-hour ride was comfortable for Crystel and Gretel because Germans rode in the coach cars. Poles rode in the freight cars, behind the engine. The luggage the Germans carried was carefully stacked in the back of the car and guarded by railroad men. Such was not the case for the Polish passengers.

Gretel stared out the window at the miles and miles of cabbage fields and only made conversation with Crystel when necessary. *Naive, am I?* she thought.

When they reached Konin, Crystel and Gretel met Herr Klein, a morbidly obese man with pronounced jowls. He flipped through a stack of papers on his desk and cleared his throat, "Weimer, Crystel, is it?"

"Yes, sir."

"Here are your papers…Wolfsbergen…you knew it as Zagorow before the occupation…head nurse."

"And you are Gretel Sennhenn?" he said as he cut the tip off a cigar.

Gretel stepped forward, stood straight and tall, and then bent her knees in something of a faux curtsy. "Yes, sir!"

She waited anxiously, for what seemed a lifetime, as he lit his cigar and flipped through more papers.

"You are going to Wolfsbergen too…head kindergarten director. When you get there, you will report to the current director. I have no more information than that. Here are your papers. Heil Hitler!"

CHAPTER 2

"**O**h! *Mein Gott!*" Crystel gasped.

Gretel was also surprised to see their mode of transportation from the Wolfsbergen train station to the kindergarten, but she said nothing. There to greet them was a gaunt-faced farmer with a horse-drawn, open wagon.

The dirty, thin man in need of a shave dipped his head politely, ignoring the deluge of rain. Water was running in a stream off his tattered, wide-brimmed hat. "I am Adel," he said with a broad smile that revealed surprisingly beautiful teeth. Adel handed Gretel a soggy note with bleeding ink. It was from Head Kindergarten Director Frau Krause, welcoming both Crystel and Gretel to Wolfsbergen.

The town had a tiny hovel of a train station, with a platform of rectangular-cut stone slabs neatly placed in a brick formation. Unfortunately for the newcomers, Adel had parked his wagon on the side of the building without a platform or walkway.

Crystel had taken just two timid steps toward the wagon, when one foot slipped into deep mud. She pulled the appendage out, but it was sans shoe, so she hiked up her gray, below-knee-length skirt and retrieved the black loafer. She tried to put it on again by balancing on one leg, but without success. Adel attempted to help by taking her arm, but Crystel pushed him aside. Instead, she took her other shoe off and splotched her way, shoeless, to the wagon.

Despite the muck, Gretel did not flinch. She ordered Adel to load their bags on the wagon. Then he covered them with some wool blankets that were in there. As if the smells of wet wool and horse droppings were not bad enough, the wagon often hauled potatoes, and the odor of rotten tubers was intense.

Adel proceeded to examine the feet of his horse, while Gretel and Crystel sat restlessly aboard the weathered green wagon sharing an umbrella. Crystel's patience level had reached its limits. "What are you *doing*?" she bellowed.

Smirking now, Adel said, "Just making sure the horse has not lost a shoe too, ma'am!" For the first time since they had left Posen, Gretel laughed aloud.

Crystel said, "I did not expect a car, but couldn't they at least have sent a covered buggy?" She stuck her tongue out and let the rain hit it. "Gretel, I think the rain is the only clean thing here! Did you see that man's hands and nails?"

"I saw them. Nevertheless, he is German, and it is part of our job to work with our people here. Those who live in Poland, those of German descent, that is, need training in the areas of health, cleanliness, timeliness, and order. They have forgotten their roots, in some cases, even the German language. They may be repatriated Ukrainians or Romanians, but they are Germans nonetheless, from generations back, and we must encourage them to change their ways."

"I know, but they live like pigs."

"If they did not live in such degenerate conditions, we would not have to empower them with the knowledge of the Reich, would we? We must teach them the importance of cleanliness and order. If we must teach them such simple things, then we must. At least here in the country, we are out of harm's way. Would you rather be in the city with the bombings? I can arrange that!"

"*Ja*, Fraulein Sennhenn, Crystel added sarcastically, "Are you going to report me now, for disrespecting your authority? *Ja*, Director? It is disgusting here! Admit it! True, we are here to continue the Germanization project, not just to care for the children of the motherland, but that doesn't mean I have to agree with it."

"I shall make a note of that. Now! You need me and I need you. We will work as a team or not at all. You are the best nurse I know. Respect my authority, and I will respect yours as head nurse."

"*Ja. Das ist gut.*"

Gretel shouted, "*Treiber! Lassen Sie uns gehen!*" and the driver urged the horse on.

After what seemed like an eternity, the wagon crested a low hill, and from there the newcomers could see what had once been a parsonage, set in a pine forest near a small, shimmering lake. The Nazis had acquired the house during the occupation, and it had undergone remodeling, including an addition, to suit the purposes of a school.

The once-proud-looking, three-story, yellow-brick house had rotting window frames, and the porch needed painting. The dormitory addition, as big as the house itself, was made of wood that was yet to be painted. The house's façade had the appearance of a square face, with a door for a mouth and windows for eyes. There were two broad chimneys, one on either end of the house roof, which stood higher than the attic apex and looked like "ears" on the "face," giving the building a comical appearance.

The pouring rain had let up, allowing the sound of children singing in unison to waft through the air. As Adel drove the wagon to the front of the house, a woman in a dark-blue cotton dress greeted them. Her build was average, except for an unusually large rear end. She shooed some chickens off the porch and addressed Gretel and Crystel.

"I am Head Director Frau Krause. I am so glad to meet you. Sadly, Frau Braun, our nurse, died of pneumonia three months ago, and as for me, I am being transferred…well, retired."

"I am Fraulein Sennhenn, the new director. Call me Gretel. You are being retired? You are not old. Forty-five perhaps? Why?"

"The party has its reasons. Younger blood is what they want."

"I don't understand. Why?"

"Introductions, Gretel," Crystel whispered.

Gretel looked visibly embarrassed. "My apologies. Frau Krause, meet Fraulein Weimer, the new head nurse. Crystel, Frau Krause."

"Please, call me Marta. Hello, Crystel. Have a seat here on the porch and I will get you a pan of water to wash your feet in."

After their quick footbaths, Marta showed Crystel and Gretel their offices. They were adequately sized rooms set in the former servant's quarters and located off the kitchen. In the kitchen were four women peeling potatoes and other vegetables. The one peeling onions wiped her tearing eyes with her apron. The carrot person never looked up, but the two other women, who were busily canning beets in the summer kitchen, smiled at Crystel and Gretel through a wall of vapor from steaming kettles.

Next, they entered what had once been an enclosed porch next to the summer kitchen. It was now an infirmary. The room had six cots that sported white sheets and hand-quilted spreads. Crystel investigated a bucket that was catching water dripping from a small hole in the ceiling. She continued her inspection by using the hem of her skirt to grasp the handle on the door of the wood-burning stove. She peeked in. "It seems it would throw enough heat," she stated.

"Right now there are fifty-seven children, ages six to fourteen," Marta said. "Most are from Berlin and Hamburg. You will get a new group every six weeks. Be prepared! They hate coming here and being away from their families; however, they enjoy the peace and quiet, as well as the friendships they make, and are equally as unhappy to leave."

To Crystel's horror, the health records, a party requirement to maintain, had had no entries for months. There were no notations for the current group since the day of their arrival. "How am I supposed to do my job? This is totally unacceptable," she muttered. "How can we show we have made progress in health and fitness if there is nothing to compare? Have they had any serious illnesses, like measles or mumps? How would I know?"

Marta shrugged her shoulders. "When the head nurse died, she had been ill for a long time. I tried to keep the records, but there was so much to do. Until now, headquarters ignored my requests for a replacement. Anyway, it is the bouts of colds and flu, which seem to come in waves that are the biggest worry right now."

"What are the immediate concerns?"

"If you are speaking about those things we deal with on a daily basis, Crystel, I would say the biggest issues are with the older ones, I would say eleven on up. The boys are experimenting with masturbation, and the girls are beginning menstruation. You will be dealing with that kind of thing often, Crystel," Marta said. "And homesickness, too."

"Oh, I'm prepared for that! I imagine there are a few that wet the bed."

"A few? That is an understatement! They come here severely traumatized by the war. There are two that defecate in their pants."

"Oh, shit!" Crystel said, with a wrinkled nose. When she began to giggle, so did Marta.

Gretel was indignant. "Enough!" she demanded. "We are professionals!"

Marta put some wood in the huge dining-room fireplace, which had once been a formal room, but now held simple long tables with church pews for benches. The former library held traditional tables where the staff ate.

Marta continued the tour by showing Crystel and Gretel the living room and parlor, which were nothing out of the ordinary.

"Get into dry clothes now," Marta said, "and I will have one of our aides, Helene, wash your things out while you take a nap. After dinner I will show you the dormitories."

Crystel and Gretel followed her upstairs to their bedrooms, which were compact but nice. Marta explained that a number of the aides shared the four other bedrooms and the attic loft.

Crystel went to her bedroom to put her things away. Marta saw Gretel to her door and turned to leave.

"Marta, please stay. I don't plan on napping," Gretel said. She stripped out of her wet things and, standing only in her undergarments, continued to question Marta. "How many aides and how many teachers are there?"

"I have that all written down for you on my...er, your desk. We have two Poles hired for carrying water, a job that takes all day. Another Polish man takes care of the garden. The aides, cooks, and laundry personnel are mostly Ukrainian. I have listed that information for you. We usually pay the Poles with food, lamp oil, and such, but we keep records of it, nonetheless. We account for everything."

"Who inventories the supplies, and where are they kept?" Gretel asked.

"I have been doing the inventory. Most of the supplies are in the empty church building behind here, and so are the classrooms. The help does the laundry and ironing there, too. It is only about seventy meters from here, but let me tell you, it is a cold walk in the winter! It used to be a Catholic church, and this was the parsonage. I will show you—"

Suddenly, there was a pounding on the front door, then the shouting of male voices, followed by heavy footsteps.

"Are you Frau Krause?" Gretel heard the men demand of one of the cooks, Emma, who had just carried in a pail of potatoes.

"Nein! I am not her!" she shrieked.

From her bedroom window, a dazed Gretel could see some children who had been outside for an exercise class being hustled back to their classrooms by their teachers.

Crystel ran down the hallway toward Gretel's room, which was directly above the main staircase, screaming, "Gretel! What's happening?"

Her shouting drew the attention of the men, German SS soldiers, who tramped up the staircase toward the room where Gretel and Marta were. Crystel dove into a hallway linen closet and hid.

Marta was crying in Gretel's room, which the soldiers must have heard because they stopped when they reached the room and kicked in the door. They immediately began laughing at Gretel's state of undress. She wrapped a blanket around herself and stood there, her eyes fixed in a horrified stare. The men were shouting over one another, and Gretel, numbed, did not comprehend their questions. But Marta did.

"*Ach der lieber Himmel!*" Marta sobbed, "I am Frau Krause. This is Fraulein Sennhenn, the new director."

"Well, Frau Krause, we have orders to arrest you for compromising the party's purpose here," said the soldier in charge. "We are to take you to headquarters. You may bring your official papers, your passport, and one change of clothes. The party has not decided, yet, what to do with a traitor like you!"

Gretel pleaded, "*Nein!* I need her help! Her advice! Don't take her!"

Marta raised her hand and gestured her to hush, "It's all right, Gretel. I knew they would come as soon as you got here. In fact, I have a bag packed already. I told you they were retiring me. That is all. I will be thinking of you."

The men took Marta away, and the last man out of the room, a handsome blonde, turned to give Gretel a "wolf" whistle and a wink.

When the coast was clear, Crystel erupted from the closet and charged like a bull to the end of the hall, where a window overlooked a porch. Gretel followed her. Four men and Marta were getting into a military car.

When Gretel tapped her on the shoulder, Crystel leaped like a grasshopper.

"Are you going to stand there all day, Crystel? We have important work to do."

"Poor Marta! She seemed like such a nice lady!"

"Appearances are deceptive. Apparently, she is a traitor to the party and compromised the welfare of the very children with which the party had entrusted her. We are without her help in the transition now. Do you see the cause and effect here? She has made our work more difficult, *Ja?*"

"Your work! My work! The party's work! Why are you are so coldhearted? Maybe she is innocent!"

"Nurse Weimer! You will go dress yourself properly, fix your hair properly, and report to my office!"

There was no answer from Crystel. Instead, she gave a huffy sigh, turned her back on Gretel, and made a beeline to her door.

Gretel entered her own room cautiously since the door was barely hanging by its hinges. She sat on her bed, trembling and twisting her hair. She sat slumped over, afraid and humiliated. However, after a few deep-cleansing breaths, she freshened up and made herself presentable to the staff.

The grandfather clock in the foyer was striking 1600 hours when Gretel headed downstairs. She met Helene on the staircase, but Helene did not let her pass by. The round-faced teenager stood pat, holding a wicker laundry basket. She seemed to be searching Gretel's face for a reaction. Gretel stared back at her, made a mental note of the odd behavior, and then broke the silence.

"I appreciate your taking care of our things."

"I do my best, *Fraulein*."

After another awkward moment, Helene let her pass.

Gretel continued down the stairs toward her office, but stopped short when she heard a chorus of weeping from the kitchen. She entered the room with her back straight and her head held high.

"Ladies! Please stop this behavior at once! The authorities will deal with Frau Krause. I know you are worried about her. However, we cannot help her situation. We will get things running smoothly again, but to do that I will need your cooperation and assistance, so please return to your duties. Dinner is at seventeen hundred hours, I assume?"

"*Ja, Fraulein,*" the onion person said.

"Thank you. I apologize for not knowing your names yet, but tomorrow, given no unforeseen circumstances, I will set up brief interviews with each of you so I can get to know you. I will be in my office if you need anything."

* * *

Gretel was sitting at her huge metal desk when Crystel peeked in.

"You look like a schoolchild at the teachers' desk," Crystel said.

Gretel bent over from her seated position to pick up a pencil. When she popped up again from under the desk, she said softly, "Sit down, Crystel."

Crystel dragged in a straight-backed wooden chair from the hallway and seated herself across the desk from Gretel. She leaned forward with one elbow on its cold, metal surface.

"They will not just retire her, you know," Crystel said.

"It is no business of ours."

"But it is! Don't you understand, Gretel? You and I are at risk of being 'retired' too, if we become resistant."

"I will consider myself warned. I forbid you to bring up the departure of Frau Krause again."

Crystel rolled her eyes. "As you say, Director! Anything else, Director?"

"*Ja.* Check the menu. It needs to include proper nutrition."

"Halt! I am head nurse! I am well aware that that is my responsibility. In fact, I just checked the menu. Do not demean me by telling me my job."

Gretel rose to her feet and approached Crystel with a lowered head. To Crystel's surprise, Gretel gave her a tender hug.

"You are absolutely right. We are both tired. It has been a long, stressful day. After we are finished with our duties, would you like to play some chess?"

"Duties! Work! Damn those dreadful words! They will not be in our vocabulary tonight. Maybe we can find some wine. *Ja,* Gretel?"

"Maybe. Let's go eat."

Simply put, dinner was a blur of activity. Gretel gave an abbreviated smile to each of the teachers she dined with, but remembered little of the introductions.

After spending some time with Crystel, she decided to turn in early, but when the grandfather clock struck 0000 hours, Gretel still had not slept. She had lost her self-confidence, her heirloom hair comb, and two chess matches, today. Worst of all, she had nearly lost a beautiful friendship. She lit an oil lamp, placed it on the dresser, and walked to the window from where earlier she had seen the military car.

It was a dark, damp, and unwelcoming view, so unlike Kassel. However, except for the occasional yowling of cats mating, it was quieter here than in the city. Perhaps too quiet. Gretel heard footsteps on the stairs, then whispering. She put a beige shawl over her white night shirt and went to investigate.

It was two of the young aides, both around eighteen years old.

"We were just switching shifts, Fraulein Sennhenn. Someone monitors the heat at all times and stokes the fire as needed."

"You have no men to do this? That will change. You girls need your rest if you are to be useful to us during the day. Besides, you cannot impress the young men in your lives with dark circles under your eyes. *Ja?* Be quiet now and I will see you in the morning."

"*Fraulein?*"

"*Ja?*"

"*Danke.*"

Gretel nodded and whisked an about-face before the girls could see the tears in her eyes.

Later, when she settled in under her warm feather comforter, her thoughts were of youth and young love. She remembered the way Wilhelm would brush the back of his hand across her cheek before lifting her chin for a kiss, and the little cottage where they first made love. Wilhelm was gone now, but not so the memories. Her body ached for him as she lay in a fetal position attempting to quell a large swell of emotions. When one side of her pillow became wet with tears, she flipped it over and fell, mercifully, into an exhausted sleep.

CHAPTER 3

Gretel awoke to the abrasive sound of nonhuman screaming. She first sat upright in bed and then rushed to her bedroom window. There was enough daylight to make out the silhouette of Adel slitting the throat of a pig. He was just inside the perimeter fence, watching the boar kick in his death throes.

Gretel lit the oil lamp, threw open the window sash, and lambasted him with angry words.

"I forbid you to butcher any animals there again! Do it behind a building or in the woods, you idiot! Clean up that mess, you filthy fool!"

"Sorry, *Fraulein*, but he got away on me. When he got stuck trying to wriggle under the fence, I made sure he didn't escape again."

"I will see you in my office!"

"Sorry, again, Fraulein Sennhenn. I did not mean to wake you."

Gretel realized that she was backlit by the lamplight, making it easy for Adel to see she was in her nightclothes. She drew the curtains posthaste.

After dressing, Gretel hurried downstairs, where she met Crystel in the foyer. She focused on Crystel through half-mast eyes and mumbled a barely audible, "Good morning."

"You look like shit!"

Gretel lifted one eyebrow. "Thanks for your support. You look fresh, Crystel. How long have you been awake?"

"About an hour. One of the boys had a huge puss-filled boil on his buttock, so I lanced it. It sure was a big, old, ugly thing."

"I thought earlier that I had lost my appetite. Now I *know* I have!"

"Huh?"

"Never mind, Crystel, never mind."

Adel reported to Gretel as ordered. When she asked where the pig came from, he explained that after the Jews had "left," the German soldiers ordered him and some other repatriated Germans to keep thieves from invading the farms acquired by the Nazis. The party had instructed them to "save all beasts from starvation." They allowed him to keep a few pigs, if he cared for them and protected the property secured during the Nazi occupation from the Poles. This, he did, in exchange for providing meat to the kindergarten.

"I make a lot of sausage. I smoke some bacon, too. The children love that. It sure isn't on the menu in Germany."

"With the rationing going on, I should say not. Where do the vegetables come from?"

"Do you think they are brought here from Germany? It is the same as with the meat. We ate the vegetables that they left behind, including the canned goods. Now we are allowed to grow what my family and the children here need."

"I see. The German race is not wasteful, and is most resource-ful, *ja?*"

Adel looked down at the floor, "If you say so, Fraulein."

"Well, from here on, try not to let the pigs escape."

"*Ja, Fraulein.*"

"One more thing. You smell awful. Next time you enter the home, I want you to wash and change your clothes. By the way, you could use a shave."

"The only razor I had was taken from me by an SS soldier a week ago, but I will do my best to find another."

It was Gretel now who spoke humbly, with lowered eyes. "I understand your predicament, but our soldiers cannot be seen unshaven or untidy."

Adel sighed and in a soft voice said, "*Your* soldiers. Yes, of course."

"You are dismissed, Adel. Oh, wait! Where is the gardener? I understand there is a Polish man that takes care of things here. Send him to me."

"Andrew? He's probably passed out somewhere again, but I will look."

"Is he ill? He should not be around the children."

"I assure you, he is not contagious, but he does vomit from time to time. He gets dizzy and has massive headaches." Adel was grinning now, and at last Gretel caught on.

"Drunk?"

"Yes, madam."

"On what?"

"He drinks the burning alcohol."

"He *what?* Adel, I thank you for being direct with me. I will find him myself. Go to work now. *Auf Wiedersehen.*"

Gretel searched the grounds. She looked behind the church, where she found a pile of abandoned Catholic artifacts. Tossed among the weeds was a statue of a bleeding Jesus, as well as a cracked fountain that had once held holy water. A thick layer of slime and mud covered them. There were also remnants of a wooden cross, which, surprisingly, no one had burned for firewood. Valuables such as the silver chalice were gone.

A chilly breeze blew, bringing with it the earthy smells of autumn. In the garden lay some squash and yams that needed harvesting. It was another reminder that cold weather would be here soon.

Gretel could not find Andrew, so she ambled toward the small lake nearby. Soggy pine needles padded the ground, muffling the sound of her footsteps. She surprised a squirrel that protested with wild chattering. It demonstrated its annoyance by flicking its tail and then scampered off.

Gretel listened to the sound of water gently lapping against the shore. Despite the smell from a dead fish that lay nearby, she took in deep breaths of air. She turned into the wind, allowing the breeze to blow across her face. It was so peaceful here that she felt guilty. After all, her parents were in the war zone, if they were even alive.

Did Wilhelm have a proper burial? Was he resting in a beautiful place like this? She would never know. What about Helmut? Gretel stood for a time in quiet meditation, twisting her hair and staring at the sparkling water.

A faint sound of a man groaning caught Gretel's attention. She peeked into a splintered old rowboat that lay ashore. She saw nothing in it but dirty water. The sound came again. This time she could tell it was coming from behind her. She turned around to see a shoeless, filthy, foul-smelling, sunburned, skinny, short man lying on his stomach.

"Are you Andrew?" Gretel asked.

He managed to say, "I am," though he was panting and looked like he would vomit. He had been lying flat on his stomach, face down, but suddenly he drew his knees up under him and grabbed his belly.

Unfortunately, for Andrew, his hind end was in the air. In a calloused, coldhearted manner, Gretel took aim and kicked him in the testicles. He let out a scream so penetrating a nearby beaver dove under water in fear.

"You had better start running, you son of a Polish sow! Get out of here or I will pour burning alcohol on your crotch and light it! You will not come near the kindergarten again!
If you do, I will not bother notifying the SS! I will shoot you down myself!"

He ran for his life, and Gretel never saw him again.

At first, the release of anger felt good to Gretel, but it quickly made her uncomfortable. Gretel had had a sophisticated upbringing in an upscale home. Her parents did not permit foul language. They were wealthier than most. Accordingly, her mother had taught her to be noticeably upper class.

Now, within two hours, she had twice let go with a spate of angry words: first at Adel, then Andrew. She was no model of sophistication now. That realization brought about a feeling more of embarrassment than guilt or sinfulness, because Gretel was not the type who worried God would strike her dead for her hateful words, or other transgressions. Gretel did not believe in God. Now, standing quietly at the base of the tree where Andrew had been, she recalled the first time she had questioned God's existence.

When she was four, a beautiful little baby who lived in the same apartment building as she had died suddenly. Gretel asked her mother, "Mamma, *gibt es ein Gott?*" Her mother assured her there was, indeed, a God, and God needed a new little angel, so he took the baby to heaven.

"I don't like God much," she had told her mother. "I don't want to go to heaven, anyway. Do people really spend forever just hopping from cloud to cloud? Helmut said so. Well, all that heavenly cloud jumping sounds boring."

She remembered how her mother had rebuked her, ordering her to hush and say her bedtime prayers. Then, as a teenager, the minister had chastised Gretel during confirmation class for questioning God and that made her turn away from religion even more.

Now, as she stood near the small lake in Poland, Gretel realized she had no time to dwell on such things, and she ran full out all the way to the kindergarten. She had wasted too much of the day.

The chilly fall morning evolved into a sunny, warm one. Gretel immersed herself in interviews, supply inventories, and routine paperwork. Despite numerous interruptions, Gretel stayed composed and professional. She was determined to get things organized to redeem her dignity.

* * *

Gretel and Crystel sent the obligatory official reports to headquarters in a timely manner, but neither one received any feedback. The party often ignored or declined their requests. The women were able to commission clothes and household goods locally, but things such as medicine or books written in German were hard to come by. Gretel complained bitterly to Crystel, and in her letters to her mother, that the high-ranking male officials did not acknowledge the sacrifices that she and other women were making, that their hard work went unnoticed. She wrote her mother:

Mamma, I was trained at Kindergarten Teacher Seminary that the best role for a woman is at home. They told us since so many women have had to go to work in the factories, that it is our lot, indeed an honorable one, to help with the mothering and nurturing of their children.

They said, "How could we ask the German troops to leave home, to fight for our country, if these men have no wife, no children, or no home to come back to when the war is over, and Germany is victorious?"

You have seen it for yourself that for many of the women, there is no permanent place to call home. When their homes have been bombed out, they depend on the generosity of those who take them in. Their children are either dead, or living away from the cities. Some women are learning their men will not be coming home at all. Yet they persist! It is only the courage and gallantry of the men that gets the attention of the officials, or the press. The sacrifices of the men are acknowledged, but not so those of the women. Women are victims, too!

Do you remember my friend Elise? She wrote me that she had to sell her body in exchange for a warm coat for her mother.

Well, winter is on the doorstep. I hope you and Papa stay warm and safe.

Auf Wiedersehen, Gretel.

* * *

November had a very solemn feel. Crystel had moved into a little cottage nearby that stood empty due to the "evacuation" of the Jewish landowners. Word was drifting in of the Nazi SS murdering Jews in the Ukraine. None of the Ukrainian aides or cooks requested a holiday anymore. It was not safe to go there.

Gretel had seen firsthand the poverty that existed in rural Poland. By now, she had heard the whisperings of vile executions, some nearby, but she could not ferret out the truth from the Nazi rhetoric. Still, she steadfastly believed the war would be over by the end of the year. As the days drew closer to Christmas, however, Gretel resolved herself to the fact that 1943 would not ring in the wonderful, peaceful year she longed for.

Gretel looked Crystel square in the eye, as they sat in front of the living room fireplace. With a solemn voice, she said, "I cannot stomach what is going on here, Crystel, but I cannot worry about the war in the broad sense, either. I have a job to do. My priority is looking after all these children. I am just one person. I cannot stop a world war."

"No. No one person can do that, Gretel. I wanted to prepare you for what was going on here in Poland, but I thought it was better you figure it out for yourself. You are very headstrong, and as dedicated as you have been to your work and the party, you would not have believed me about the vile things that go on. Now that you know, just watch your own ass. That is all either of us can do."

Gretel prepared the school for a Christmas celebration, but without any joy. She had the children at the school make little presents for the repatriated Germans in the community. Her job required her to teach these children to sing Christmas carols in German, including the well-known *Silent Night, Holy Night.*

Members of the military hierarchy would be visiting, and Gretel would see to it that the children were well prepared to entertain them. The evening would be a combination of Christmas rituals; but to please the party, it would include the observance of the winter solstice and speeches touting Hitler rhetoric. Hitler's picture, not a Nativity scene, would be the centerpiece of the dessert table.

The Christmas Eve performance came off exactly as practiced. Gretel stood tall, her back straight, as she directed the little children's choir. She sang along with them—"*Schlaf in himmlischer*

Ruh!"—but she knew full well that for people all over the world, there was only the sleep of death, and there definitely was no heavenly peace on earth. If there was a heaven, she thought, it must be at war, too, for God was obviously too busy to stop the one here; and if God were to be the final judge, how would he make mankind pay for such egregious sins? Gretel could only wonder.

The grandfather clock in the foyer struck 0200 hours as Gretel walked up the stairway to her room, a place where she did not have to feign holiday joy. She lit her lamp, took out some paper, and began scrawling some words. After numerous attempts, she was at last satisfied with the results.

> *There is no war to end all human strife.*
> *The only war left now, could end all human life.*
> *Never-ending peace and brotherhood of man,*
> *Is but a dream, a wish, no more.*
>
> *Nations rise and reach for power.*
> *They trample down their neighbors' rights,*
> *While striving to obtain what is not theirs to take!*
>
> *Leaders cry out, 'the only way to live is ours!'*
> *Their bloodstained hands lifted up in prayer,*
> *As they make vain appeals to gods of war.*
>
> *Let the leaders take the weapons in their hands!*
> *Then peace would settle over all the lands!*
> *They have a controversy. Let them fight!*
>
> *No, this is folly, for The Conqueror remains,*
> *His plans for ever-greater power are first of all.*
>
> *Flames, again, are flaring up on far horizons,*
> *While the songs of brotherhood and love,*
> *Are trampled under marching soldiers' boots.*

Gretel folded the piece of paper in three and gently put it inside an envelope that held Wilhelm's last letter to her. The postmark read, "20/07/1942." Was it five months or a lifetime ago? So much had changed in that short time.

* * *

By the summer of 1943, Gretel had arranged for the installation of electric lights. She hired a local Polish man named Jakob to do the electrical work. Though they spoke few words to one another, Jakob had a way that charmed Gretel. Under the circumstances, she had to pretend she did not notice his frequent glances.

On one occasion, Gretel asked Helene to find Jakob and send him to her office. It was the second time that day. "I have a question for him," Gretel said.

Helene gave a disapproving sideways glance. "And what question might that be?"

"I didn't ask him which room he will be working in tomorrow."

"I am surprised you forgot to ask. I will ask him for you, *Fraulein.* I'll save you the trouble."

Gretel realized now that Helene was suspicious of her intent and was toying with her.

"Well, yes, you could ask...but I need to reprimand him for taking too long."

Gretel had obtained seven starched white aprons from a German man who ran a restaurant that once belonged to Polish Jews. Now she fumbled through a box for them, then quickly bundled them up and handed them to Helene.

"I just realized something. I thought it might be nice for my aides to wear these. It would look so professional. Please distribute them, Helene. I will send someone else to find this man

Jakob. It might take a while to find that lazy Pole. I will not keep you."

Gretel was annoyed with herself, because she certainly did not owe Helene any explanation. In most cases, her verbal responses to the staff were brief and routine. Why was she so flustered? What was it about Helene that chafed her so? Gretel could not put her finger on it.

Helene and the other aides did have some organized recreation, but at ages seventeen and up, if they snuck off with their boyfriends, there was not much Gretel could do. To ensure they did not, she would have had to follow them on their days off and late at night. She never chastised them for coming in late, as long as they were able to perform their duties the next day. She envied their giggles and whispers and wanted to be included in their conversations, but it was not appropriate.

Sometimes, in between groups of children, the staff had a few days' respite of their own. It was during those breaks that Gretel made frequent visits to the little cottage where Crystel now lived. It was there that Gretel confided in her friend that she missed having the love of a man. "It has been so long since I was with Wilhelm. It was May Day last year," Gretel said.

"That's rough, but wasn't it you who said the war would be over soon?"

"Screw the war! Screw the lies! Screw the wonder weapon! It feels like the fighting will never be over! I feel so old, Crystel. I am twenty-seven, not that much older than some of the aides. I have desires. Do you know what I mean? Someday I want to marry and have children."

"Lucky you."

"What are you trying to say?"

"Gretel, it has been three years for me since I last had sex. I won't ever be able to have children, even if I could find a man who wants me."

"That is so silly. You will fall in love again, once this war is over. You are very attractive, you know. You and your husband never had children, but you were only married a short time. You could have children with someone else, I'm sure."

"I told you my husband died of a ruptured appendix. It is not true. I left him because he gave me a venereal disease."

"*Und kinder?*"

"*Nein. Ich bin steril.*"

Gretel looked at Crystel with sad eyes and reached out to give her a hug, but Crystel pulled away.

"Ah, Gretel! I never meant to tell anyone. I guess I had a weak moment. Let's not talk about it. Do you want some schnapps?"

"Where did you get it? Yes! I do!"

Gretel wanted to cry for Crystel, but instead followed her lead. They both got drunk…and sick. They toasted each person they knew who had died in the war, and after each one shouted, "Salute!" They cursed the war and the men who ran it. They cursed the men at party headquarters for ignoring their requests and for treating women as second-class citizens. When Crystel said Hitler was such a big asshole that his wonder weapon could be "shoved up it," Gretel broke into a fit of maniacal laughing and consequently peed in her pants.

In the winter of 1943, despite Crystel's warnings, Gretel began secretly visiting Jakob, and she spent time with his family, too. They were disowned landlords; in fact, they were descendants of Polish royalty, highly educated and spoke fluent German. Jakob's parents were polite to Gretel, but uneasy about the relationship.

From their first meeting, Jakob's appearance awed Gretel. He had dark hair and was short like her. His clothes fit loosely, as he had once been heavier, but even now, he was not thin. He was not the Aryan ideal, but she found him so handsome she knew she would not resist his advances if he wanted her.

On one beautiful moonlit December night, they decided to go horseback riding. Jakob lifted Gretel onto his horse and climbed on behind her. He wrapped his arms around her at chest level, his hands covering her breasts. When Gretel expressed no resistance or embarrassment, he slid forward, pressing his thighs tight around Gretel's hips.

Jakob first put the horse into a canter, to warm his muscles some, and then urged the gelding into a trot. The snow was deep and powdery, and the air was cold, but still, so the horse and riders were very warm. Without warning, Jakob kicked the horse into a full gallop, and the animal's mighty legs kicked snow out from under him as he ran. Before long, the horse was breathing heavily. With each pant came a billowing of vapor from his lungs. The bodies of the lovers rocked forward and back, in tandem with the motion of the horse.

When they got back to the barn, Gretel was not surprised to see a blanket spread out on the hay. On it lay a small bundle of anise cookies tied up in a handkerchief.

Jakob's lovemaking had a way of making Gretel forget all else. It was not wild and playful, as with Wilhelm; it was gentler, easier, like a narcotic that numbed the pain and fear of war. She savored every touch, every kiss, memorizing it as if it were their last. If someone caught them, it would be.

CHAPTER 4

In the spring of 1944, the war escalated in Poland. An increased German military presence meant frequent patrols in the area. Gretel's visits with Jakob became much more risky and fraught with perilous consequences.

The ripple effect of the war changed life at the kindergarten, too. Instead of groups of 50 or 60 older children coming for six weeks, the party assigned 160 German preschoolers there permanently. The oldest children were five, the youngest ones, two. Many were orphans, a result of the March eighteenth British attack on Hamburg, where more than three thousand bombs were dropped.

"They will arrive on the fourteenth of April," Herr Klein had told Gretel. "I am assured you will handle this assignment well, Fraulein Sennhenn. These children are Germany's future; they are important to the survival of the German people. Heil Hitler!"

The next day, while recalling Herr Klein's words, Gretel paced the floor of her office. In a conversation with herself, she touted, "I am the only head director the bosses trust with such young ones! This war, and my work here, will soon be over, and I will be able to get superb job recommendations!"

Crystel overheard her and peeked in the office door.

"Herr Klein must have given you a bunch of butt kisses!" Crystel shook her finger at Gretel. "I will not let you feed off that snake slime of a man! Those children are coming here because the party does not know what else to do with them. We do not factor in; you have said so yourself."

Gretel blushed and looked down at her feet, "Yes, yes, you are right." She bit her nails and paced even faster. "Oh! We have so much to do! We can tolerate no disorganization. I must instruct the helpers to finish their work assignments. Crystel, tell the cooks to be prepared. *Die lieben* will be hungry when they arrive."

"If you would quit gloating for a minute, you would notice the papers I put on your desk. I have set things in motion, already. The cooks have outlined some menu changes. They gave me some good ideas."

Gretel flipped through the papers and gave an approving nod. "Those women are very wise. You are too! We will do a good job in spite of the party, not because of it!"

"*Ja*, we will, Gretel."

After dinner, Gretel became restless. She had to alert Jakob that she could not see him, for perhaps weeks, because it would take time until the initial chaos was resolved and the kindergarten operated efficiently again. She felt compelled to run to Jakob, but instead walked slowly on the one-kilometer journey to his house. If the Gestapo saw her, she would feign innocence by telling them she needed a long walk to collect her thoughts before the young children arrived. The soldiers would believe her because the story was verifiable.

Gretel looked side to side, and over her shoulder, but saw only the glowing eyes of a raccoon in the near darkness. The military rarely patrolled these roads until a few months ago. Now, the Nazi soldiers traveled about the countryside pillaging and raping. They shot Poles for sport. To gain favor with the Reich they killed Germans for alleged or even minor offenses. Those considered traitors, such as Gretel would be, were often tortured first.

When she reached the limestone, thatch-roofed cottage Jakob shared with his parents, Gretel stood motionless, squinting in the semidarkness. She could still make out Jakob's wagon. He had parked the battered-looking but sturdy rig to the east of the carriage barn. In this way, he signaled Gretel to meet him at their secret place.

Gretel did not follow the driveway to the barn. Instead, she kept low, maneuvering her way along the shadows of the many trees there, skulking her way past a row of recently pruned gooseberry bushes. When she reached the wagon, she positioned two stones on the left side of the driver's seat, signaling Jakob to meet her at 0200 hours.

Gretel turned to leave, but stopped dead in her tracks when she heard a distinct rustling sound and something that sounded like breathing. Her pulse raced as she ran toward the road, trying her best to retrace her footsteps. She brushed against one of the gooseberry bushes, and it scratched her leg. She could feel it bleeding, but did not look down.

Once she reached the road, Gretel forced herself to walk nonchalantly. She dare not appear to be doing anything shady.

Everything had to appear normal at the kindergarten, too, so at 2230 hours Gretel wished Crystel, "*Guten nacht*," and waited in her room.

As she lay there, imploring the grandfather clock to strike 0100 hours so she could leave, her thoughts ran rampant. Those sounds she'd heard at Jakob's carriage house must have been the horse Baroque, she reasoned. He must have been nearby, standing by the pasture gate; she just hadn't seen him in the dim light. Was that it? No, it was not. She did not hear Baroque snort or whinny. More than that, Jakob always put the horse in the carriage barn well before dark, then bedded and fed him.

Each evening before retiring, Jakob checked the wagon seat for Gretel's signal. It must have been him she heard breathing, Gretel theorized. Surely, he felt something was amiss and did not want to draw attention to Gretel by saying anything. With that, she let out a tentative sigh of relief.

Gretel dozed in a seated position on her bed, not daring to lie down lest she fall fast asleep. The midnight clanging of the grandfather clock snapped her wide-awake. She began reading her copy of Shakespeare's *A Midsummer Night's Dream,* but did not comprehend the words. Her thoughts focused only on Jakob.

At 0100 hours, Gretel put a coat on over her nightclothes. If someone at the kindergarten saw her moving about, she would say she had insomnia and was going outside for a breath of fresh air.

Gretel peeked through the keyhole and then quietly turned the doorknob. She opened the door very slowly. Seeing no one, she abruptly, but ever so softly, closed it again and changed into a blue blouse and a gray jumper. She reluctantly donned the one expensive piece of jewelry she had left, a pendant with an aquamarine stone set in silver. If the patrolling soldiers stopped her, it might be necessary to bribe them with the jewelry. She would have preferred to use her antique hair comb, but it was still missing, having vanished on her first day at Wolfsbergen

Jakob had arrived first. He greeted Gretel with a wet, tender kiss. When he sat down with his back against the base of the tree, he turned her around so that she faced away from him. All in one motion, Jakob gently slid his hands up under her skirt and pulled her down onto his lap. She did not turn around to face him. Instead, she let her body relax in his arms. Gretel closed her eyes as Jakob began kissing her neck. She could feel both the softness of his lips and the roughness of his whiskers. She knew by his breathing that he was aroused.

"You cut your hair. It's nice," he whispered. Gretel sighed softly as Jakob reached around her waist and slid his hands between her thighs. Suddenly, she stopped him.

"I have something to tell you."

"Oh! The lady plays hard to get tonight," Jakob said. He pushed his body firmly against hers so she could feel his erection.

"Stop that, Jakob! I have important news."

"Tell me, Gretel."

"You know that I've been waiting for the next group of children to come."

"*Ja.*"

"Herr Klein called. He said one hundred and sixty children, ages five and under, will be sent here"

"You'll do just fine. You meet every challenge head-on."

"You don't understand! I cannot see you for a while. I will not have the time. More helpers are on the way, but that also means more paperwork. I have to retrain my aides to work with small children. Oh, I just remembered! I'll have to find someone to build some potty chairs!"

Jakob began to laugh aloud. Gretel pulled down her skirt and turned around to face him. "Do you think this is funny?"

"No. I just cannot picture what that will be like…all those young ones. You caught me off guard."

"I love you, Jakob, but I have so much to do to prepare. This must be our last night together for a while. Do you understand?"

He answered only with his body. This time Gretel responded so passionately, so completely recklessly and with such abandon, that Jakob must have sensed something apocalyptic in her mood.

When they finished their lovemaking, Gretel began to sob in despair. She managed to choke out the words, "I'll miss you."

They had been lying on Jakob's shirt. He gently wiped Gretel's tears with it and said, "I will not try to contact you until the first week of May."

They finished dressing and kissed a dozen times. Jakob pulled away from the embrace. "Go now, Gretel," he said. "You need to get a couple of hours' sleep. I love you!"

He turned away, but Gretel grabbed him by his suspenders. "Never forget me, Jakob. No matter what happens. Do not forget me."

"Never."

As he walked away, Gretel could hear him crying.

On April fourteenth, Gretel and her staff waited for the train. "Make the children feel welcomed," she said. "Wave and smile when we see them."

The smiles did not last. The "future of Germany" was a herd of dirty, tired, hungry, homesick ragamuffins. Many had nothing but the clothes they wore. Some wore soiled diapers, and others had vomited on themselves. Crystel flashed Gretel a look of alarm when she noticed oozing sores associated with impetigo.

Gretel stopped herself from twisting her hair and blinked away tears. Her mouth gaped open. She could not fathom how just three nurses handled their 160 charges for the entire two-day trip. What courage and strength they had!

This time Gretel did not stand as tall as possible, nor did she use an authoritative voice. Her shoulders were relaxed, her voice quiet, her demeanor humble. She thanked the exhausted chaperones, individually, by name, and then dismissed them to find a hotel where they could bathe, have a meal, and get some much-needed sleep.

"Do, please, have a safe trip back to Germany," Gretel said. "But first, ladies, I have something for you." She dug deep into the canvas bag she carried and handed each woman a bar of perfumed soap from her personal stash that her mother had sent when she first came to Poland. The gift was highly prized by the women since the only soap available now was foul smelling and rough.

The kindergarten staff escorted the weary little travelers to the dining room. "Don't worry about bathing them yet," Gretel said to her assistants. "Just have the children wash their hands and get them fed."

The county nurse was late in arriving. Crystel was frantic. Gretel went to her office to place a phone call. "She's on her way? She will be bringing extra help? *Danke!*"

Once the help arrived, Gretel, Crystel, and the county nurse checked each child, and deloused those who needed it. It was necessary to quarantine the ones with impetigo. Ten helpers spent the rest of the day giving baths and disinfecting clothes. By nightfall, the staff had given these hapless victims of war one more meal and put them to bed.

Kindergarten teachers from other villages stayed the night to comfort the little ones who cried inconsolably. Most worrisome were those in a state of shock and noticeably numb to their surroundings. They showed little emotion. Such tiny, psychologically fragile innocents required special care.

"I need an aide to work with them only," Crystel told Gretel. "Especially little four-year-old Thomas there. He won't talk."

"Did he used to?"

"Yes. They found him next to his dead mother after an air raid. Someone stole her shoes as she lay dying in the street. The last thing he said to a neighbor woman who took him in was, 'Mamma has no shoes on.' Then he shut down."

Gretel had turned away to go to her office when Crystel tapped her on the shoulder. "They're all blonde and fair-skinned," she whispered. "Did the Nazis cull out which ones they wanted to come here? They are Aryan looking. What happened to the others?"

Gretel stopped her. "Please do not bring it up again, Crystel. It is not safe to talk about it; and for that matter...I don't want to know."

That night, in her private quarters, Gretel allowed herself a good cry. Shortly after she fell asleep, a knock at the door woke her. It was the aide Klarysa. "The nurse, Frau Weimer, she needs you. Four of the children have fevers," she said.

"Oh my!" Gretel knew that fetching a doctor wasn't possible; the doctor came only once a month because he had to travel twenty-five kilometers by horse-drawn buggy. "We will have to handle this situation ourselves. We must take care of these unfortunate children, no matter how tired or overwhelmed we feel, Klarysa. They need us. You know that. Don't you?"

"*Ja*, Fraulein Sennhenn."

"Good. Leave me to dress. Tell Crystel...Nurse Weimer...I'll hurry."

* * *

By autumn the adult food rations throughout Germany (mandated by the German government) had shrunk to six potatoes, one tablespoon of butter, a half pound of meat, a quarter pound of cheese, a loaf of bread, and a half pound of dried peas or beans a week; children got more. Every two or three weeks, the government permitted them two eggs each.

However, those at the kindergartens in occupied Poland had a bounty by comparison. They received food, including eggs, from the farms run by repatriated Germans, and there was no rationing of vegetables, which were plentiful. The fall canning season was now over, so unlike in Germany, the shelves at the kindergarten were full of delicious food.

Now, chilly rains were frequent, a prelude to still another winter. Gretel was sitting in front of a blazing fireplace, towel-drying her hair, when she heard a cough and heavy wheezing. "Fraulein Sennhenn, is it true?"

"Klarysa! You startled me. Is what true?"

"I am so sorry, *Fraulein*, but the cooks are putting the untouched leftover food in a pail outside the fence. Some Polish children come to get it. The other aides are whispering."

"Do not worry yourself, Klarysa. I told the cooks to do that."

"*Das ist verboten!*" Klarysa said, between gasps of air.

"I am aware of that, but I am tired of seeing the poor little ones begging while good food is wasted. They are Polish, but they are still children, and winter is just weeks away. Do not fret. If the authorities find out, there will be no blame directed at you, or any other of my aides. You are not involved. Now, these cold fall storms cause your asthma to act up. Go to the nurse, and ask her to let you rest in the infirmary for a time."

"*Fraulein?*"

"*Ja?*"

"I like it very much that we have running water in the kindergarten, now."

"Me, too. It sure made it easier for me to wash my hair. Now, go. Take a rest."

Gretel pulled her chair closer to the crackling fire and ran a comb through her wavy hair. The Polish children Klarysa spoke of, the so-called "misfits and miscarriages," had been hanging around the fence for weeks, stealing morsels of food from the garbage pails. They wore ragged clothes and no shoes. Their matted hair seemed stuck to their heads, which looked out of proportion to their skinny bodies. Their dull-looking eyes had dark circles under them. When Gretel had first noticed their infected rat bites, she wept openly.

A cold dampness crept into the kindergarten, but the thoughts of those children made Gretel even chillier. She wrapped a green knitted afghan around her shoulders, but after just a few moments, removed it, folded it again, and put it back in the blanket chest. How selfish such comforts seemed when so much suffering was going on.

The beggars at the fence were the children of a Polish woman whose husband the SS had arrested weeks earlier. She had no way now to support her nine children. The oldest was twelve, the youngest just two months. Without the food, the older children would die. If their mother did not get some nutrition, and soon, she and the nursing infant would die, too.

Gretel had learned the background of those children from the county nurse, who defied the party and went fearlessly, along with Gretel, to the homes of Polish women to deliver their babies.

"What a shame the Polish children live so," she had told Gretel. "At the same time, the German children at the kindergarten are too full to finish the food on their plates."

Gretel had pressed her lips tightly together and clenched her fists. "It is risky, but I have to do something," she had said. "What good would I be when the war ends if I have learned to insulate myself from feeling?"

She still remembered the soft touch on her shoulder the woman gave her as she uttered the words, "God be with you, Gretel."

Gretel had surprised herself by answering, "With you too, Marlis."

It was only two weeks after Gretel gave instructions to feed the Pole children, that the party called Gretel to the office in Posen.

"Good God, Gretel!" Jakob gasped, when she told him. "Are you in trouble?"

"Absolutely not."

"Remember, Gretel, Frau Krause was arrested and never returned!"

"Exactly my point. They *arrested* her, and she knew they were coming! They are not coming to arrest me. Herr Klein and the others are asking me to come to Posen for some meetings, and that is all there is to it. I should expect to be there for just two days."

"My darling Gretel. You are so naive! You have helped deliver the babies of Polish women and have fed their children. If word has gotten out, those men will not hesitate to kill you! Besides, you are making me crazy in love with you, and I want you every minute, but this…you and me…it is dangerous! I am not some-one of German descent who happens to be living in Poland. *Ich bin Polnisch!*"

"We have talked about that many times. We agreed to focus only on the future. The war will be over soon."

"I pray so, Gretel, but the Soviet troops are at the border. Poland will not be under Nazi occupation much longer. The Allies are coming! It is dangerous for you to be here with me for that reason alone. What you are doing is death defying, and it would be even if you were not resisting the Reich, which you are."

"Listen to me, Jakob. They are most likely sending me still more children; some are orphans, poor things. That would take some expert organization, and they know I can do it. The bosses need my input."

"So, you'll go there to lick the boots of these cowardly men at their request?"

"Don't humiliate me like that! To them, I am just a woman, and they own me! They force me to prostitute my mind and soul to them if I want to live! I would only hope they do not ask me to prostitute my body as well. They know who my parents are. Do you get the picture?"

Gretel placed her fingertips on Jakob's cheeks and looked him in the eyes. "I will play their game as long as they wish. I will go there, all right, but I will be back in a few days." She gave Jakob a dispassionate kiss and left abruptly. He appeared relieved. An emotional good-bye would be too draining for either of them.

While Gretel was leaving instructions at the kindergarten, Crystel walked about nervously with a worried expression. "Something is not right about this. They normally request you come to Konin regarding the kindergarten. Why would they choose Posen this time? Why headquarters? Do you think they know?"

Gretel dropped her inventory list. When she bent over to pick it up, she felt dizzy and her heart pounded. How much *did* the party know?

"If they know about the feeding of the Polish children, I'll just deny it. They cannot prove a thing. I will tell them we put our garbage pail outside so Adel can slop the hogs with it. I will say the Polish children may have stolen some of it; however, I was not aware," Gretel said. She volunteered no further discussion. True to her belief that the less one knew the better, Crystel did not bring up Jakob.

While on the train to Posen, Gretel listened to the discussions of the other passengers. They spoke of U.S. troops reaching the Siegfried line (West Wall). The Americans were there to defend the allied countries of Belgium, Luxemburg, France, and Holland. This was not good news for the Axis powers! Even so, the West Wall lay west of Germany, and Poland was east of

Germany. Gretel reasoned that since the battle was so far away, neither she nor the other passengers were in immediate danger.

Gretel closed her eyes so she would not appear to be listening to the conversation. It was safer that way.

"And since the first of August, there has been terrible fighting in Warsaw, too!" one woman said. A tall man in a handsome suit answered, "Yes. The stupid Poles are in some kind of revolt, but their army cannot hold off the superior German troops much longer. Our brave soldiers have depleted the Polish army. They will soon surrender. Now be quiet, you foolish woman!"

* * *

Each time Gretel arrived in Posen, she felt as if she were stuck in time. There was the same gray, imposing City Building. The same stern woman with rigid posture sat at the desk in the foyer. There was still the dim lighting in the hallway to the boss's office and the same strange odor of a cleaning solution.

When Gretel entered the boss's office, he left her standing in the middle of the room for several minutes. He did not speak and did not look at her. When he finished sharpening his pencil, he turned to face her. Gretel could see he was furious. His next words sliced into her mind with a sound as harsh as a chainsaw hitting metal.

"So! As to you! How far do you think you can go, sabotaging the party?"

The blood drained from Gretel's face, and her hands became sweaty. Did he know she fed the Pole children? Did he learn she gave milk to a Polish woman whose baby was dying or that she helped to deliver Polish babies? Perhaps he knew she listened to foreign radio broadcasts. He could not know about Jakob, of that she was sure. It would have been grounds to kill them both on the spot.

Whatever he knew, Gretel hoped the party boss would go easy on her. She had purchased him black-market items, such as nylons for his wife; then there were the wine and expensive cigars she gave him to gain favors.

In a snarling voice he asked, "You! Tell me! What business do you have defying the party?"

Gretel refused to fall for the familiar trap in which she would relate to *him* what she had done. Some people during questioning blurted out such things as, "I only listened to the music when I turned on the foreign broadcasts!" By doing so, they sometimes admitted to things the party was not aware of. Gretel was resolved that he would have to tell *her* what he knew.

"You have no right to accuse me of anything! I have done nothing to deserve such treatment!"

"Look now! I have been informed that you have been feeding the ingrate Pole children!" He deliberately bent over to look Gretel straight in the eyes. "You would deprive our own children to do this?"

"No, sir! I did not feed the Polish children!" Gretel stomped her foot for emphasis. "The children at my home are not deprived; in fact, they are some of the fittest and healthiest in all the kindergartens! You have said so yourself on your visits there."

"Get out of here! Find yourself a place to sleep. I will deal with you in the morning! Heil Hitler!" He crossed the room and slammed the door behind him.

Gretel took a deep breath for the first time since she had arrived and walked double-time down the hall. An SS captain caught up with her.

"You need some rest after your long journey. Follow me, *Fraulein*. I will show you where you can stay," he said. He helped Gretel on with her coat and chatted about the weather. He carried her suitcase and opened doors for her. Not until they reached the basement of the City Building did Gretel know there was a jail down there. *They were arresting her!*

CHAPTER 5

The once-welcoming SS officer gazed down at Gretel's horror-struck expression and smirked. With his left hand, he reached around to the back of her head and grabbed her hair; then, with one sharp motion, he pulled her face into his chest. He used his baton in his right hand to strike Gretel lightly and superficially across the back. It was a blow meant to get Gretel's attention, not injure her; still, she yelped in a reflex reaction.

The captain opened the cell door. In it were two cots, two chairs, two dirty towels, and an open pail that served as a toilet. When he shouted at Gretel, "*Sie Dirne!*" it shocked her, only because it was the first time anyone had called her a whore. "*Sie Dirne!*" he said again, and then shoved Gretel into the jail cell, putting one of his feet in front of her as he did.

She landed on her hands and knees, and looking up from that position, she noticed a woman sitting on one of the cots. A tacky mass of dried blood pasted her hair to the left side of her head. She gulped air like a guppy out of water, causing Gretel to suspect the anguished woman had cracked ribs, internal injuries, or both.

Gretel could focus only on the woman and did not notice that the SS man had unzipped his pants to expose himself. Her mind did not register the sound of his laughter, or the high-decibel marching music blasting over the loud speakers. There was antiseptic in the toilet pail to disguise the odor of urine and feces, but she did not smell it; nor did she feel the cold or the dampness in the basement. It seemed all of her senses, except her vision, had gone numb. Gretel knew that if she came out of this situation alive, she would never forget that sight: a woman beaten nearly to death.

"I will return shortly," the officer said. "I will need to inspect your papers when I get back."

When he left, Gretel tried to make conversation with her cellmate. "I'm Gretel. You seem to be injured. What can I do to help?"

The woman sat mutely on the bed with her hands behind her on the naked cot, obviously attempting to stay in a seated position. Her breathing was distressed, so much so, she could not bend forward or lie down. Propping herself up in this way allowed her to breathe easier, Gretel realized. She wanted to help, but there was nothing medically she could do. The woman's death seemed inevitable and her fear nearly palpable.

Gretel noticed that the dazed woman's gray, hand-crocheted socks were stepped down into her loafers, and she offered to help pull them up.

"Oh! That must be uncomfortable," Gretel said. "Don't you just hate it when they slide down like that? May I pull them up?" Although the woman did not respond, Gretel knelt down and proceeded to fix the footwear problem.

A clanging noise and a male voice brought Gretel up off her knees. It was the same guard. "You would not get down on your knees before that woman and attempt to help her if you knew she murdered one of our finest SS men! On the other hand, you probably would, whore!"

In an instant, the man's formerly blasé demeanor transformed into a vile, savage one that Gretel had never seen before. Her voice quivered when she asked, "She killed him? Why?"

"He was one of our elite, and he only wanted her affections. To oblige him would have been an honor! She got the treatment she deserved, but you obviously feel sorry for her. I will recommend to my superiors that you receive the same punishment!"

Gretel took a defensive posture: "If you think I care about her dilemma, you're wrong. I have enough troubles of my own. I was hoping to collect the socks off her feet if she died, but they have holes, so I do not want them. If looking at the socks is a crime, I committed one. As far as I am concerned, you can take her out of here. I do not give her an hour to live. Why should I sit here with a dead woman?"

The man's chameleon-like face switched now, from an angry expression to one of amusement. "You certainly are a scrappy whore!" he chuckled. "As you wish, *Fraulein!*"

When the captain yanked Gretel's cellmate off the bed, the woman let out a high-pitched squeak from the very top of her trachea. Taking a deeper breath was impossible. Gretel took her by one elbow, pretending to assist the soldier in removing her, but in a subtle gesture, she squeezed the doomed woman's hand gently and apologetically.

Once they left, Gretel sat silently on her cot, trying to justify her self-serving actions. The ever-present marching music, Hitler rhetoric, and Nazi-adulterated news were pulsing from the speakers, but otherwise the jail was still.

It had been hours since Gretel ate, and she was feeling weak. Eventually, she heard the sound of a door closing, then footsteps. A guard with a much heavier build than the first man appeared and introduced himself as Lieutenant Hinkley. He set a slimy, dirty, wooden tray on the floor. Next, he removed a ring of keys from his belt loop and unlocked the cell door. Gretel could see the tray held a sandwich and an enamel bowl containing a brown liquid. Hinkley told her not to waste one drop of it.

"Enough of it will turn you brown on the inside, the proud Nazi color! Perhaps our generous meal will make traitors such as you better Nazis! Now, *drink!*"

Since there was no flatware, Gretel lifted the bowl to her lips and took a tentative sip. It was a thin onion soup with no salt.

Obediently she drank all of it. "Thank you," she told him, lest she get nothing more to eat. The rest of her meal was a lard sandwich on very old, dry bread. It gagged her, but she finished it nonetheless.

The drain of the entire day was beginning to take its toll. Every part of Gretel's mind and body were vulnerable. Her attempts to rest were futile, because the sounds of marching music and slanted military reports on the radio never quit, and visions of the beaten woman haunted her. The vile, metallic smell from a puddle of blood left on her cot and the smell of her urine on the floor where she had stood were nauseating. Gretel tried to read a book she had packed in her suitcase, but her mind played tricks on her, causing an illusion of white letters on a black background. Since the guards had stolen her watch and the jail had no windows, Gretel did not know what time of day it was, or for how long she had slept, until Hinkley approached her.

"*Guten Morgen, Fraulein!*"

"Good morning to you, Lieutenant."

He unlocked the cell door and placed the same dirty, greasy tray on the floor. On the menu were another lard sandwich and more of the plain, watered-down onion soup. She flicked a rat dropping off the side of the bowl and began drinking the polluted-looking potage.

"Finish quickly," Hinkley ordered. "The party boss wants to see you."

He waited until she finished, then made ready to take the tray away.

"You will be questioned soon, and that may take some time. Do not tell anyone I warned you, but you best use your pail while I am gone. Then I will show you where to dump it. I am not such a bad person, you see."

"Yes, sir. I appreciate you being so kind as to forewarn me."

"I assume you will tell the *kommandant* how efficiently I work, and that I deserve a promotion. *Ja?*"

"*Ja*, Lieutenant."

One dim light bulb hung from the ceiling in the room where Lieutenant Hinkley led Gretel. The only window had a dark piece of fabric draped over it. This looked nothing like the party boss's office. Gretel's head pounded and one eye had developed a tic. The boss had said he would see her in the morning in his office. Right? Why did the guard lead her to this scary room where there was blood on the floor?

Gretel bit her lip when the reality hit her. This was a place where prisoners were beaten! This was where they interrogated criminals! She had done nothing as horrific as killing an SS officer! She was no criminal.

There were four SS officers, one in each corner of the room, and barely visible in the dim light.

"Leave her to us," said one voice.

"I believe we can handle a short little mouse such as her," said another.

"*Ja, Wohl!*" Hinkley said, then snapped an about-face and left the room.

One man dragged a stool to the middle of the room, under the lone lightbulb.

"Be seated, *Fraulein,*" he said tersely as he held the stool for her, but when short, petite Gretel started to hop up onto it, he pulled it away. Gretel fell to the floor, landing on her buttocks spread-legged. He picked her up, slammed her down on the stool, and returned to his seat in the corner.

"So, you admit you fed them!"

Gretel cringed at the sound of this man, who had a much deeper voice than the other interrogators.

"Fed whom, sir?"

"*Die polnischen kinder!*" he shouted.

"*Nein!* I did not feed the Polish children! I can say that with all honesty!" (It was true, after all, because they were not asking if she had *ordered the cooks* to do it.)

One man, barely visible in the dim, shadowy space, lit a cigarette. As he held the lighter to his cigarette, it illuminated his face like a jack-o-lantern. Gretel could see he had a gray moustache.

He asked, "Why do you lie? Our sources say you fed those vomited discards of the Polish race! How dare you endanger the health of our own German children by giving them less than enough to eat!"

Gretel attempted to flatter his ego. "Why, sir, I understand you have a job to do, and the SS plays a vital role in the very plan our beloved Fuhrer has outlined; however, someone has told you an outright lie that is keeping you from more important work."

He bolted from his chair and slapped Gretel sharply across the face. "I am never kept from any important work! Not by you or any other imbecile! I will not let the likes of you determine what my priorities are! Now! Did you feed the Polish children?"

"No, sir, I did not."

The deeper voice shouted, "Hinkley! Get in here!"

Hinkley, who had been guarding the door, entered the room, snapped to attention, and said boldly, "*Ja, Wohl!*"

"We are going to take a break," one of the men said. Gretel was feeling woozy, so it was not clear to her which one was speaking. "You, Kindergarten Director Sennhenn, will sit facing the corner until we return! You behave like a child. Don't you think children who lie need punishing, *Fraulein?*"

"Yes, sir, but I didn't—"

"Shut up! We are going to take a break. You will not speak until we return! Is that clear?"

Gretel dared not speak, so she nodded her head.

"Hinkley! Put the stool in the corner. See to it that she does not get down from it. You will not allow her to speak. These are your orders."

"As you wish, sir!"

It was Hinkley, now, who sat in the darkened area of the room. After a few minutes, he spoke. "Do not turn around, *Fraulein*, and whatever you do, don't say a word. They did not say *I* had to be silent, so I will give you some advice. Admit what you did. You may lose your job, but if you do not confess, you could lose your life. Don't you see? The SS does not have the time or patience for this kind of thing, and denying it will just anger them."

Gretel sat in silence, remotely aware of a stinging sensation on her face, the sound of footsteps on the floor above her, and the smell of cigars infused in Hinkley's wool uniform.

When the SS interrogators returned, the party boss was with them. This man, who had been friendly to Gretel over the years and to whom she had brought black-market goods, acted as if he had never known her. He addressed her as, "Hey you!" "Traitor!" and "Look now, woman!" though he knew her name well. Each time he spoke, his breath belched the odor of sardines.

For days, it was the same routine. The lack of food, sleep, and fresh air, along with endless hours of badgering, caused most of the incarcerated to become confused and numb, so that even the innocent prisoner eventually would confess. Such punishment was standard Nazi routine, and Gretel knew it.

For Gretel the worst thing was the lack of sleep. The SS men would slap and hit the offenders just enough to make them bruised and sore so they could not sleep. In addition, the constant noise of the marching music took its toll, as well as dehydration and malnutrition, which made some people hallucinate.

Gretel knew their tactics and managed to stay focused just to spite these wicked men. As the days went by, things became tolerable because she was emotionally numb and no longer cared what they would do to her. The hunger pangs went away, but now she could not eat without gagging, and she was getting weaker. The only upside to that was being able to sleep more.

Every day, during the hour long interrogations, the SS men asked Gretel if she fed the Polish children, and every day she denied it. At one point Gretel giggled, because no one ever asked if she gave orders for someone else to feed the Polish. For giggling and because she would not tell them what was so funny, the men stuck a dirty sock in her mouth.

Each day, Gretel made a point of saying how she feared Hinkley, and could they "please assign another guard" because he frightened her. She said no guard could do a better job than Hinkley.

On the tenth day of her incarceration, Hinkley woke her. He had Gretel's coat in his hand. "I have orders to let you go. There is no explanation," he said. He helped Gretel on with her coat and carried her suitcase up the stairs. When they turned the corner, the stern woman at the front desk stared Gretel down. Hinkley did the same, and then shouted, "Get out of here! And take your lies with you!" With excessive dramatics, he dropped Gretel's suitcase on the floor and left.

When Gretel got outside, the cold air made her sniffle, so she put one hand in her coat pocket to find her handkerchief. It was then that she felt something sticky and pulled it out. She was amazed to find a fresh piece of strudel wrapped in newspaper.

Gretel purchased her train ticket, but it would be an hour until the train came. She sat on the same park bench she had the very first time she was in Posen and on every visit since. As she ate her strudel, she noticed there were no pigeons and no old woman selling rolls. No longer did the people feed the pigeons; now the pigeons fed the people. The birds must have been a feast for the people, compared with eating cats and rats. The elderly lady with the rolls was probably long-since dead, and most likely, Gretel thought, no one had shed a tear for her.

Gretel found a phone and called the kindergarten.

"Hi, Crystel. I am on my way back. How are things?"

"I'm glad you called, Gretel. What time will your train arrive?"

"About fifteen thirty hours. Have Adel pick me up."

"Adel is dead."

"Oh! No! What happened?"

"I will send someone for you. I have to go now."

Crystel's blunt response was a crushing blow. What happened to poor Adel? How were things at the kindergarten? If she were not so weak and tired, she would have fretted more, but Gretel slept all the way to Wolfsbergen.

A man named Rolf met Gretel at the train station. Gretel recognized him as the man with unusually hairy hands who ran the grocery store in Wolfsbergen. "I have a delivery for the kindergarten, so when Fraulein Weimer asked me to pick you up, I said I would."

Gretel put the suitcase on the wagon, unassisted by Rolf, then climbed up onto the wagon's bench seat and pulled the lap robe over her legs.

"I have a lot of rutabagas and onions with me. You best dig a root cellar if you haven't already."

"We have one. Rolf, I know that you dealt with Adel frequently regarding supplies for the kindergarten. I understand he is dead. What happened?"

"Don't you know, *Fraulein*, that the more often a bit of information is repeated, the more chance there is for misinterpretation?" He remained reticent, belched, and said nothing more.

Gretel was growing uneasy. She sat quietly, occasionally sighing or twisting strands of her hair. Suddenly, everything seemed to be in a state of disorder. Would Jakob want to see her, or would he feel it was too risky? How did Adel die? Crystel had brushed off any questions about Adel or the kindergarten. Why?

Once at the kindergarten, Gretel walked in and placed her suitcase on the floor in the foyer. The aide Klarysa saw it and picked it up.

"I will take this to your room."

"I am glad to see you, and very glad to be back," Gretel said.

"Ma'am," Klarysa said somberly with a polite nod, and then she climbed the stairs toward Gretel's room.

Gretel panicked. Why was everyone behaving so strangely? She ran to Crystel's office. Crystel glanced up from her desk.

"The Nazi soldiers shot Adel for treason, then they took little Thomas away to an asylum; necessary, they said, since he could not speak."

"Not Thomas! No!" Gretel screamed. "Is it my fault? Is any of this my fault?"

"I am sure it wasn't anything you did."

Gretel got the dry heaves, and sobbed so hard in between retching sessions that she passed out. When she regained consciousness, she kicked away the pillows Crystel had placed under her legs and sat up. Crystel led her to the infirmary.

"You have not eaten much, have you, Gretel."

"*Nein.*"

"I will get you some broth, but you should have nothing heavy on your stomach for now."

"*Danke.*"

When Crystel returned, she attempted to spoon-feed Gretel.

"I can do it. Crystel, what happened to Adel?"

"Finish your broth, rest a little, and then come to me. I need your help."

Gretel slept fitfully; in her dream Thomas was falling...falling... then something from the abyss swallowed him up. When Gretel woke, she could smell lavender. Helene was sitting on the cot across from her, drenched in Gretel's perfume and wearing the antique hair comb that had been missing since Gretel's first day.

"You did not sleep long, *Fraulein.*"

Gretel wobbled a little when she stood up. Then she eyed Helene with a fierce expression. Helene lay back on the cot with her hands behind her head and smiled. Gretel shook her finger at her. "You wretched thief! I will report you for stealing my things and see to it that you are fired! Stand up when I address you!"

"You must be tired, so I will save you the trouble of asking. *Ja, Fraulein!* I was the one who reported you to party headquarters for feeding the young Polish degenerates! I did not involve the cooks or Nurse Weimer, because they only followed your instructions. It was your blunder, not theirs! I was the one who recommended Thomas go to a sanitarium, because you failed to do it! *Und ja!* I revealed that Adel was interfering with the repatriation project, and that is why he is dead. I still may tell them about you and that ingrate Pole, Jakob!"

"So! You were the one who had been following me! I should have realized."

Helene remained lying on her back, her hands behind her head, only now she lay spread-legged in an unladylike fashion.

"Whenever the mood strikes you, come to my office, Helene," Gretel said. She fled the room, holding the waistband of her skirt, which, like most of her clothes, was loose now.

Gretel sat at her desk, numbly looking through the pages of notes Crystel left her: Someone has been stealing supplies, so Gretel would have to match the supply list to the inventory. Heidi, a seven-year-old, was having night terrors. Daniel, age four, was showing signs of allergies to something outdoors. One of the aides, Catherine, was pregnant, and there was no one nearby who could "take care of it."

Gretel put the papers down and tearfully forced herself to open Thomas's file. She made a notation that read, simply, "Removed," then went to Crystel's office with Helene on her heels.

"Crystel, is my mail in here?"

"Yes, I will get it."

"Fraulein Sennhenn!" Helene said in a smug, arrogant tone. She held up a spice bottle. "Look what Rolf brought me! It is caraway seed for the rye bread and sauerkraut. We have been out of it for so long! I am sure you are extremely grateful. *Ja?*"

"As was Rolf, I'm sure, when you had sex with him, you brazen sow!"

"Now, *Fraulein*, a person's private life should be kept private. I am sure you agree with me. Obviously, there are times when there is a need to expose an affair…"

"She is incorrigible, just ignore her," Crystel whispered to Gretel as she handed her the mail. Gretel noticed a dull appearance to Crystel's eyes and a drawn, gray look to her skin.

"Are you OK, Crystel?" she asked.

"As well as I can be under the circumstances," Crystel muttered, while tilting her head toward Helene. It was a reminder to Gretel that the newly exposed Nazi informant was listening.

When Gretel left to return to her office, she noticed the house cat had left the vomited remains of a rat on the floor. Her mouth opened to say something to Helene, but instead, she cleaned it up herself.

Within a day, Gretel had the kindergarten operating in its usual rhythm—with one exception: Helene propped her feet up on the couch and did nothing. The other aides took up the slack and did the work normally assigned to Helene. As the staff walked back and forth, Helene took copious notes, of no importance or value, except for intimidation.

The threats about Gretel's affair had put a strain on her relationship with Crystel and might have caused the two women to lose their grip on their friendship, except that they would not give Helene the satisfaction.

When the two found a moment alone, Gretel apologized. "I am so sorry, Crystel. What you must have had to deal with while I was gone, I cannot imagine. Adel, Thomas, and that *Dirne* Helene! What more?"

"I agreed we should feed the Polish children," Crystel said, "so some of what happened is on my shoulders, including your arrest. Who knows? If I thought any man would want me with my venereal disease, I might have pursued the idea of an affair myself, but we have work to do, and we can't change what Helene knows."

It was noon on the third day after Gretel's return when she walked out past the perimeter fence in the direction of the woods. One of the children was sick, and the others had said she ate some mushrooms that grew there. Gretel examined the loose dirt and found a few more mushrooms. Fortunately, they were harmless ones.

Gretel was making her way back when she looked up to see Jakob. He was out on the road, appearing over-involved in adjusting the harness of his horse and inspecting the wheels on the wagon. The two cautiously eyed each other as if indifferent. Then, he nonchalantly hoisted himself onto the wagon and left. Knowing Helene could be anywhere, Gretel calmly washed the dirt off her hands at the outside pump and returned to work as if nothing had happened.

Gretel set to work inventorying the canned goods. For the third time since her arrival in Wolfsbergen, the canning season was over. Another autumn was nearing its end, signaling the winter to come: the winter of 1944–45. She counted the many colorful jars of fruits and vegetables and took note of the dozens of empty canning jars. They should have been full of canned meats such as chicken, pork, or beef, but Adel, and the meats he cheerfully and faithfully provided, were gone.

Gretel learned from Crystel that Helene had exposed Adel for helping his nephews escape from one of the Nazi-run camps designed to discipline and "reeducate" Polish children of German dissent—that is, those who refused to be sculpted into "appropriate" Germans in favor of maintaining their Polish heritage. The SS men shot Adel point-blank, stole his cigarettes and much of the food in his house, and then continued on with their corrupt mission.

Helene had also bared Frau Krause's plans to hide two such Polish children. Their parents had resisted the efforts of the Nazis to indoctrinate them into "Germandom," too. In retaliation for such disobedience, the Nazis commonly kidnapped, raped, or even killed the offspring of the defiant parents. For all her heroic efforts to save these innocents from harm, they arrested Frau Krause—her fate unknown.

In early December, the party reassigned Helene. She left with almost everything of value that Gretel had and with no guarantee she would not reveal the secret of Gretel and Jakob.

Then came a surprise. Gretel received orders to send all the children back to Germany and to release the aides for a month long holiday. Gretel's status with the party was tentative, so she did not question why, but assumed a new group would arrive in January.

The events of the past weeks had not curbed Gretel's voracious appetite for sex with Jakob, but instead made the hunger in her loins more intense. She wanted desperately to see him, hold him, and know that he still loved her. Jakob had no legitimate reason to come to the home for repairs or deliveries now that the children were gone, so she would have to go to him. She set out on foot for Jakob's place.

CHAPTER 6

Yearning made Gretel plod on to Jakob's farm. Though it was a scary venture, she fought her fears as she stumbled along in near-total darkness. Because the snow, paired with an unrelenting wind, helped fill in her tracks, Gretel trekked on, unabashed by concerns that the patrols would spot her.

She slipped into the barn, prepared to wait for Jakob as long as it took. Baroque snickered and whinnied, but did not seem unduly alarmed by her presence. He nuzzled Gretel with his velvety-soft nose and might have smiled, if a horse could. Gretel laid her head against his warm neck and promised him that next time she would bring some sugar.

Jakob would be there soon to bed down Baroque for the night, but the walk to Jakob's farm had been punishing, so Gretel blew into her icy hands, then grabbed a pitchfork and fluffed some straw in the corner of the barn that was the least drafty, where she succumbed to her exhaustion. Soon, a hand brushing as soft as a baby's breath across her nipples interrupted her peaceful sleep. She stifled a gasp and shook in terror until she recognized Jakob's silhouette in the dim lantern light.

"I wanted to come sooner, Jakob, really I did, but Helene…"
Jakob lay beside Gretel to keep her warm while she detailed the
whole story of Helene's betrayal.

"I knew it was something like that. God knows I never wanted
to be the cause of any harm to you."

When Jakob kissed her, Gretel began to chuckle. "You taste
like wine," she said.

Jakob laughed, too. "It is dandelion wine, aged to perfection.
My mother makes it better than anyone I know."

"I should go and have a visit with her soon. I have not seen
her in weeks," Gretel told him.

Jakob pulled her face close to his. Speaking softly, but firmly,
he said, "Gretel, I am sure my mother and father would love to
see you, but your being here makes them nervous. I heard the
party ordered you to return the children to Germany; well, I want
you to leave Poland, too."

Gretel took off her coat and lifted her blouse. Exposing her
left breast, she said, "Put your lips here. Now feel my heartbeat
and listen to it! You are here, inside my heart, always! I would
rather die than go back to Germany without you!"

Jakob pulled her blouse down and helped her put her coat
back on. "Haven't you heard the distant rumblings over the last
three days? It sounds like thunder."

"Yes, I hear it occasionally, if the wind is the right direction."

"The Russians have crossed the border. They are only a few
kilometers away. It is tanks you hear, and battles."

"The Russian army is busy fighting battles in the cities and
towns, but they will not come here, Jakob. What would they
clash over in this rural area? Some rundown, abandoned farms?
Perhaps they want to pick a fight with the laborers and the peas-
ants? Maybe they want to collect the rotting corpses of dead
Jews?"

"Gretel! Sarcasm doesn't become you."

"I'm sorry. But really, there is nothing here they would be
interested in."

Jakob stood, pulled Gretel into a standing position, and shook
her shoulders. "Damn it Gretel! You are so incredibly naive!

Germans! They want Germans! They want to put all of your people on the run! They want your people out of Poland!"

"My *people?* That is probably the most insensitive thing you have ever said to me! I will not go! Do not ask me again, because I do not have the authorization to go anywhere. I am waiting for the party to send me the next group of children."

There was nothing left to say, so Jakob held Gretel close. She could feel the tenseness in his muscles, and when she reached for his hand, she could feel he had bitten his nails to the quick, something she had never known him to do before. They held each other in an embrace, still with that searing yearning for one another, but they did not make love. The mood had vanished. They commiserated for another hour or so until the snow let up a bit, after which Gretel made her way back toward the school. This late at night, when the weather was bad, the soldiers were usually holed up in an abandoned house somewhere in a drunken stupor, so she was not afraid.

When she was near the kindergarten, Gretel saw a dim light on in the abandoned house Crystel had moved into, so she stopped at the house and gave the door a gentle knock. When there was no answer, Gretel opened the door. Crystel was lying on the floor, passed out drunk. Gretel turned her on her side, in case she vomited, and covered her with a blanket. A half hour later, Crystel showed signs of waking up, so Gretel washed her friend's face with cool water.

"Leave me alone, Gretel! I don't need your meddling!"

"Since when is caring about you meddling? If I had not stoked the fireplace, you would be near dead with cold. What's gotten into you?"

"The war is upon us now. The Russians are very close, and the German army is losing ground. We will have to leave or be killed, Gretel. There are signs all around, and I am scared."

"I'm scared too, but I know there is something more. You are a mess! What's wrong?"

"If we get out alive, what will you do?"

"Go back to Kassel, of course; hopefully with Jakob."

"But what would you do there?"

"I would see my family first, then find a new job and get married, maybe."

"*Ja!* You have your family and you have Jakob. You still have a chance for love and children, if not with him, with someone else. Most of my family is dead, and no man would want me. When I leave here, I will have no home, no job, no one to go to, and love is out of the question. You can't possibly understand!"

Crystel became excessively emotional and despondent, so Gretel knelt on the floor next to the weakened soul that had once been her prideful, strong-willed confidant and comrade, and gently stroked her hair. Crystel looked at Gretel with squinted red eyes, then wiped her tears and said simply, "*Mein freund.*" Although it was their most intimate moment, they never spoke of the episode again.

During the next days, Crystel dutifully sent supply requests to headquarters in preparation for the next group of children, but she received no response. Gretel and Crystel spent most of the lonely, cold winter evenings together, and the county nurse joined them on occasion. But their discussions grew stagnant, and their mood wavered between melancholy and outright fear, sometimes masked by nervous laughter. Gretel's phone calls to headquarters only invited annoyed voices that oozed tension and anger, so the women waited.

Crystel and Gretel spent Christmas quietly. They took the smallest tree they could find and decorated it with bows made from cloth scraps, pinecones, and garland made of popcorn strung on sewing thread. It was enough. They exchanged homemade gifts and sang songs of tradition, but the Christmas spirit had vanished.

Gretel continued to see Jakob, but on a less-frequent basis. Their trysts were usually in the barn, but they sometimes met at the old oak tree, just to stand there, hand in hand, as they longed for warmth, sun, and a soft bed of leaves to make love on. Meeting at the kindergarten was out of the question. They did not want to involve Crystel or the now-skeleton staff of Polish workers who did minor repairs and heavy lifting and cut wood. Gretel's and Jakob's disobedience was of their own doing, and perhaps it would be their undoing, but their love, wounded by fear and uncertainty and stitched back together by hope for the future, could only survive if the war did not rip their sutured souls apart.

On New Year's Day 1945, Gretel was virtually blindsided by news from Jakob. "My parents want you to come for dinner," he said.

She had only to step inside the doorway to sense that Jakob had coerced his parents. What was so important that they would risk having her visit? The Nazis had forced Jakob's family, descendants of Polish nobility, from their original home. They were well-educated people, fluent in German, yet Jakob's mother whispered to her son in Polish several times during the meal, an act considered ill-mannered by most. Gretel planned to excuse herself once they had finished washing the dishes, but suddenly an awkward silence fell over the group. Jakob took a dishtowel from her and dried her hands with it.

"Gretel, you don't know how close the Russians are to driving the German army home, clear across Poland! I wish we could help the Germans drive the Red Army back to Russia, but your Hitler sees only traitors in us. We do not want Communists here anymore than your people do! I want you to pack quickly and go to Kassel. I would try to come with you, but I have to stay here until we have enemy contact."

The family grew quiet, as if in anticipation of something. Gretel's jaw went slack and her mouth dropped wide open when Jakob pulled a ring from his pocket.

"It belonged to my grandmother," he explained. "If we both get out of this war alive, I want you to marry me. And mind my words: Germany *will* be defeated."

The ring fit perfectly. Gretel gave Jakob a modest kiss and promised to marry him. Trembling, she hugged his mother, and said, "I will treasure the ring. Thank you for a lovely meal." Jakob held Gretel's left hand tightly as she shook hands with his father. "Sir," she said, and gave a slight curtsy.

An engagement, a suggested trip to Kassel, and the defeat of the German army were almost too much for Gretel to absorb at one time. She and Jakob made love in the barn that night, but Baroque was restless and distracting. Even he seemed nervous. However, it was when Jakob offered to walk Gretel home, despite the risks, that she, for the first time, became anxious.

When Gretel was in her room again, she took the ring off and examined it closely. There was engraving on the inside, but she could only make out the year: 1864. The stone was a deep-green tourmaline with the coat of arms belonging to Jakob's family engraved in gold. The ring was a beautiful thing to behold, and the engagement was thrilling, but the war and its companion—uncertainty—diminished some of the joy that would otherwise surround such a moment. Oh how she wished she could tell Crystel! Out of charity, Gretel would keep the engagement a secret; the news would be just too painful for Crystel.

By late January, Jakob was unrelenting about Gretel leaving Poland. He repeated his plea, again and again: "I don't want you to die! You have to leave *now!*"

It was no fun to think of a cold two-day trip in an unheated train, she had been telling Jakob since mid-December; the party would just send her back to the kindergarten again when the next group of students was due to arrive. Besides, there was no alarming news over the radio, and the little town of Wolfsbergen was several kilometers away from the main roads the German troops were using in their flight from the Red Army. All was peaceful. She saw no reason to leave.

"Besides, if we die together, it will have been an honorable love," she said.

At first Jakob ranted in Polish, then he switched to German, shouting, "*Dieses ist nicht Romeo und Juliet! Sie stummer Kopf!*"

"I am not stupid! How dare you, Jakob?"

"How dare *you* assume I want to die? We are lovers, yes, but you would not stick a dagger in your chest for me, nor I for you. You have to be realistic. Go! I will get my parents back to the home they had stolen from them during the occupation, and join you in Germany later. We will get married then, but I cannot join you if you are dead, and you *will* be dead if you travel with a Polish man!"

Gretel continued to disregard his pleas until one bitter-cold morning in the later days of January when further news arrived. It was minus twenty-six degrees Celsius, so in order to conserve the wood it would take to heat the entire building, Gretel had slept in the empty infirmary. The heat from the pot-bellied stove was her only salvation from freezing. She was barely awake when Jakob barged in the front door bellowing her name. "Gretel! Hurry! Get packed!"

He was not asking this time. He demanded she get her things together and ordered the Polish workers to ready a wagon for the next morning. "Feed the horses well tonight!" he screamed at them.

The ever-skeptical Gretel called the office in Konin. There was a recorded male voice: "This is your emergency operator. Communications with Konin are severed! Try calling the office in Posen." Then silence. Gretel tried to reach Posen, but there was no answer.

Satisfied that she understood the urgency, Jakob shouted, "I'll be back, Gretel!" and scurried out the door.

Within minutes, a messenger came with a letter from the village commissioner. All Germans were to pack, it said, and in the morning, drivers would meet them and escort them by wagon to the train station. Jakob had already heard! What he said about the inherent danger was true. Her much-maligned naiveté had overruled common sense once more.

Gretel dressed quickly and ran to Crystel's house. Her lungs ached from breathing cold air, and the moisture in her nose made her nostrils feel frozen together. Even from a distance, Gretel could see there was no smoke coming from the chimney, and that worried her, so she ran faster. She did not bother to knock on the door, but shoved it open like a brutal intruder.

The house was viciously cold, and it was obvious Crystel had left hours before. The sight of her clothes strewn about, along with a half-eaten box of candy and a bottle of wine left on the table, triggered a throaty moan from Gretel. Crystel must have left in a panic. Why else would she leave such scarce items behind? Pure kismet had brought them together after so many years, but now the very war that reunited them would separate them once more.

Gretel took a swig from the wine bottle and toasted Crystel aloud. She shoved two pieces of candy in her mouth and then ran around the entire perimeter of the house to be sure Crystel was not lying somewhere injured or freezing to death. Only the lonely cottage and the memories of her friend remained, so Gretel returned to the kindergarten. It was time—time to go.

The rest of the day was a blur. Gretel sent the Poles home loaded with food, made some sandwiches, and then packed her clothes, books, and bedding. She burned all records concerning the children and some of her own records, as well. By nightfall, she had packed two big trunks and several smaller suitcases. She filled one small suitcase with valuables and important things, such as her bankbooks, passport, and money, along with a change of underwear, a washcloth, soap, and towels. As an experienced traveler, she knew it was vital that she keep this most important satchel close to her.

Jakob failed to return to the kindergarten that day, so Gretel made her way to the little house he shared with his parents. The house was empty, leaving Gretel to surmise he was taking his parents back to their homestead, now that the German army could not stand its ground there. Though the Germans who confiscated much of their belongings would be gone from the house, Jakob's family was determined to defend it against continued ruthless marauding from others, just as he said they would do.

She checked the barn. Jakob's wagon and Baroque were gone. If only he had returned to say good-bye. Gretel searched the house once more, but found no one. As she turned to leave, she noticed something carved into the wood on the entrance door. It was a message from Jakob: "*Gretel! Ich finde Sie!*"

Yes, he would find her someday, and it would be a beautiful, emotional reunion. Of these things, she was certain. Nevertheless, today she would experience no swell of emotions and no tears, only numbness. She would move on to stay alive for him. The myriad of events that brought them together suddenly seemed vague in Gretel's mind, as if already in the long-ago. Soon her sojourn in Poland would be over.

Gretel spent the evening in wistful contemplation, but with the daylight came overwhelming sights, sounds, and smells. There were dozens of horse-drawn wagons lined up and down the road, and such a confluence of people (mostly Germans) she could not count the number! The evacuees were frightened, some were crying, and all were unsure of what was to happen. Mothers shushed their children, promising they would be home soon and all would be well. As they sang lullabies to their babies, their breath formed white plumes that dissipated into the bitter wintry air.

One wagon had been loaded with Gretel's things, minus the small satchel she guarded carefully. On top of the pile was her bicycle. An enormous stash of other suitcases sat on the same wagon. They belonged to a woman with four small boys.

In this subzero weather, they, and all the other exiled Germans, had no blankets! Without blankets this mass of humanity in this haphazard wagon train would freeze! The Poles still took orders from the Germans, so Gretel hollered to some of the wagon drivers, "Get all the blankets from the kindergarten! There are one hundred and sixty beds with two on each bed, and I want every one of them! Distribute them quickly!"

A fleeting pang of guilt touched her, because most of the blankets were procured from the Poles during the invasion and afterward. Gretel was herself guilty of taking fabrics, clothes, and kitchenware from the empty homes of Polish Jews that had been "evacuated" by the Nazis. Now a network of disparate emotions scuffled to define her character. "I was ordered to supply the kindergarten," she muttered to herself, "I had no options." One fugitive tear ran down her cheek before she resolutely stomped her foot. "Hitler caused this war, not me," she reasoned, and then she readied to leave, absent any shame.

In the distance were the sounds of military vehicles and gunfire! Was it the Russians? Was it Germans on the run? Was it both?

Rogue soldiers from the Ural Mountains of Russia, loyal to General Vlassow and allied to the Germans, acted as their escorts. These impromptu marshals aimed to keep the drivers from unhitching the horses and riding back; but when their purpose was finished, they would be on the run, too, considered traitors by the mainstream Russian army. They were a slender, dark-haired, Mongolian type of people with fur caps, dark-blue uniforms with red trim, puffy breeches, and high boots. Riding on small, swift horses, they carried bayonets, their appearance reminiscent of men on a World War I battlefield.

The procession lost its bearings and drove in circles all that day and night, then the next day and night and into the following day, without reaching the train station. Any food brought along was frozen and useless. Gretel warned anyone who would listen not to put the frozen food next to his or her body to thaw it, because doing so would drop their core temperature even lower than it already was. The best they could do was to build a tent of sorts with the blankets as a shield against the merciless wind.

Before long, so many wagons had joined the procession, the roads were jammed. Gretel put her head in her hands and rocked back and forth. It was the first overt sign of stress she had shown.

Unexpectedly, one of the soldier escorts tapped Gretel on the arm with his whip and pointed at her Red Cross armband. When he motioned her to come, she hesitated, so he deftly lifted her off the wagon and onto his mount. Someone needed her help, that much she knew, but she did not speak Russian. They galloped along until they came to a small cottage where he opened the door and pushed Gretel inside. Her eyes met those of a fair-skinned woman with a twisted expression, about to give birth. When the soldier sat cross-legged on the floor, adjusting his position so he could get the best view, Gretel flashed him a disapproving look, but he just grinned.

Within minutes a premature little girl, tiny but perfect, was born. Gretel toweled and warmed her with a flannel shirt that was there. The baby cried lustily as an elderly woman who was with the mother kept watch for her to deliver the placenta.

Gretel placed the baby on her mother's chest, but she did not immediately begin to suckle, so Gretel reassured the new mother that the infant would eat soon. The old woman nodded in agreement. The warm water felt good on Gretel's cold hands as she washed them, so she took her time at it while she spoke to the mother. "What will be her name? Do you know yet?" Gretel asked.

"I had other names in mind, but it is Gerda," she answered. "It means guarded and protected."

"I understand. May angels guard her and protect her," Gretel said, knowing that without such a miracle, the newborn could not survive such woebegone conditions.

The old woman handed Gretel a pencil and a piece of paper. She wrote on it the mother's name, home address, and the baby's time of birth. Below that she wrote, "*Born on the trek,*" and then signed it. This would be little Gerda's birth certificate.

The soldier gave Gretel a swig of whiskey, which burned like hellfire in her empty stomach. When she gasped, he laughed, and then he hoisted her onto the steed again. He mounted the horse behind her and deliberately slid his hand up and down Gretel's thigh near to, but not touching, her groin. Even a week ago, she would have protested such overt sexual contact from anyone but Jakob, but dignity and pride did not seem to be valid virtues amid such despair. Instead, she ignored his behavior and began to prattle on about Hitler, the Nazis, their lack of contrition, and the wicked chain of events they had triggered. The soldier, who did not understand German, leaned to one side and turned his body to see her face, then looked at her with a puzzled expression. Gretel shrugged her shoulders and said nothing more as they rode back.

Gretel wondered if she would be able to find her wagon among so many, but the crowd of refugees had not been able to move one meter all the while she was gone! The roads were jammed with damaged wagons, collapsed from the weight of the people and their belongings. The ditches became vessels for broken-down wagons and abandoned luggage. Stranded people frantically tried to get on any wagon that was still in one piece, but were refused or beaten away. Some were relieving themselves by the roadside, and little boys did not even bother to leave the wagons to do so, but as bad as things were on this insane exodus, these conditions were only the bellwether of things to come.

Gretel was hefting herself back onto her wagon when suddenly the brain-chilling sound of machine-gun fire rang out in the distance. As feared, the Red Army was catching up to them! Panic erupted, and the Vlassow escorts fled. Many of the Polish drivers, with no one to stop them from doing so, unhitched the horses and rode them back to their homes. The wagon Gretel's things were on was still in good shape, and the driver stayed with it—but for how long?

When she heard no more gunfire, Gretel eased herself into a standing position. From this vantage point on the wagon, she could see in the distance a small train. Smoke belched from it, so she knew the engine was operational. Most likely the train had stopped to take on coal for fuel.

"I think I could make it," Gretel said to Marie, the woman with the four small boys aboard the same wagon as she. "I might have enough time to get there before it leaves. If I take only my bicycle and my small bag, I could cut across the field and be there in ten to fifteen minutes."

"No! Gretel did you say your name was? Gretel, we need you. I could use your help with the boys. Please? The train will leave before you get there, and there will be no room on it, anyway."

Gretel observed the three-year-old boy Marie was holding. At first glance, he appeared to be asleep, but then she noticed his yellowish, waxy-looking face, bluish lips, and eyelids that were half closed over staring, broken eyes. Gretel did not tell the mother the boy was dead. Instead, in a squeaky, auxiliary voice, she said, "Good luck to you!" and albeit awkwardly, bounded off the wagon.

She retrieved her bike and the highly valued small suitcase, and then headed toward the train. Attempting to catch it was a risky maneuver, but the sun was setting, and it was now or never.

When she was halfway to the train, Gretel heard several petrifying blasts. In a spontaneous reaction, she looked back. A violent enemy attack had blown up some of the wagons, including the one she had been riding on. Brain-chilling screams from the wounded filled the air. The silent people—the dead ones with missing heads or limbs or eviscerated torsos—were probably the better off, Gretel reasoned. She vowed not to be another victim and rushed on to reach the train.

Once there, Gretel bribed the engineer with a bag of home-grown tobacco meant for her father. He helped her into the box-car and loaded her bike and her bag. Without more ado, he blew the whistle, and the little train chugged off.

It would be the last small-track train out of the area and the only rail transport to a larger train service, because the railroad men had set dynamite on the tracks behind them and detonated it to disrupt the lines of transportation from the east. It was, liter-ally, the region's last train west.

CHAPTER 7

Gretel moved forward to one of the passenger cars. Surprisingly, there were only a few hastily bandaged soldiers and some railroad men on it. She nestled into one of the grimy seats where, as luck would have it, someone had left a blanket. Using her valise as a pillow, she fell fast asleep.

She had not eaten in so long that her dreams were more like hallucinations and her sleep was very close to a state of unconsciousness. She envisioned Crystel on the coast of Spain, sitting in the warm sun, laughing. "I warned you to leave earlier, Gretel. Naive! You could have been here with me. Naive!" she was saying.

In her dreams, Gretel also saw Jakob in a Red Army uniform. He was galloping toward her on Baroque and screaming at her to run for her life, to leave Poland at once, and he was firing a gun in the air!

Gretel jolted back from her nightmare to realize the gunfire she was dreaming about was real. There was a skirmish nearby, but fortunately, none of the bullets hit the train and it chugged on.

She reached for the ring Jakob had given her. It was beautiful, and so was their love, but was it only for a season? Too exhausted to deal with such deep emotions, she dozed off again.

It was midnight when they reached the next stop, Kustr, where Gretel switched trains. It, too, had only a few passengers, mostly refugees and soldiers. Gretel tried to eat her sandwiches, but they were still as hard as stone. A soldier sitting opposite her was eating lard from a can with his fingers. He offered Gretel some of it, but just the sight of the dirty, greasy stuff forced her to look away. He smirked and prophesied, "Given time, you will eat anything." He told in gory detail of a dog roast he and some other soldiers had when they were at "The Front." The conversation taxed Gretel's limited strength, so she ignored him. Without an audience, the soldier said nothing more.

The plan to destroy all the tracks behind the train continued. It stopped often, for long periods, while workers strategically placed more explosives. Shuddering blasts from detonating dynamite announced each departure.

At one stop, there was an angry turmoil in the next coach. A woman was yelling, and a hostile railroad man was bellowing, "Give it up, lady, or get off the train!" Gretel leaned out the window to witness a pitiful sight. The woman was screaming hysterically while clinging to a large package. At first Gretel failed to understand why anybody would get so excited about leaving the box of goods behind, as it was better to travel light. "I just wanted to give my child a proper burial!" she bawled. "Why can't I leave the box tied to the door?" There were several more verbal exchanges, mostly his heated words followed by her pleading. Eventually the woman fell silent and walked away from the train station, still cradling the box.

For the first time since leaving Poland, Gretel allowed her tears to fall unchecked.

* * *

It was sunny when the train reached Posen, where it sat for hours. The wind had died down, and the warmth of the sun beating on the train made the temperature inside it tolerable. By now, there were hundreds of people on the train, and all cars were nearly full. Many passengers got out looking for water and food, but there was nothing.

Gretel was no longer hungry because her system was shutting down for lack of food. She was lightheaded, her thoughts distant and hazy. Everything seemed surreal, but the meaning of the conversation she overheard when she walked outside the train was clear.

Two railroad employees and three soldiers were in a huddle. Gretel moved closer and nonchalantly eavesdropped. They were discussing what to do because Russian tanks were just five kilometers west of Posen. "Berlin? *Nein!*" said one man. They agreed the train would have to go south and eventually cross one particular major bridge. If it were still intact, they would blow it up, disrupting the advancement of the Russian army. Many Germans still believed Hitler to be omnipotent and that Germany would win the war after all, and these men were no exception. "Our Fuhrer would approve of our plan!" the smallest soldier declared. In unison the men responded, "Heil Hitler!"

Out of habit, Gretel opened her parched mouth to respond in kind, but this time the words attached themselves to her tongue, as leeches, and she could not, would not, say them.

If not Berlin, where would the train end up? Gretel did not know, but someone motioned her to get aboard the train, so she grabbed a handful of snow, ate it, and returned to her seat. The railroad men bailed out of their huddle when bullets hit the train with a fierce tat-a-tat and a steely whine. The vibrations from the gunfire were so loud they shook the train, and those who were still outside it catapulted themselves aboard. The whistle blew, and the train left Posen, a town Gretel had come to despise.

For the entire afternoon, the train rumbled on through timber, fields, and more timber. People on overloaded wagons, on foot, or pushing bicycles loaded with luggage were visible at the clearings. Sometimes they would attempt to jump aboard the moving train. A few athletic soldiers made it successfully, with the help of passengers, who would pull them into the doorways as the train slowed down near each village. It did not come to a full stop anymore, not at any station.

At nightfall a blaze on the horizon, apparently a village set on fire, became visible. Passengers craned to look out the window in awe. The train crossed the railroad bridge, and as planned, the explosives were set in place and ignited, destroying it. The travelers cheered. One woman wept. "Perhaps we are safe now," she blubbered.

Gretel shivered uncontrollably, despite a double layer of clothes, slacks, a scarf, and ski boots. It was too cold to sleep, so she occupied herself by honing in on a debate between the two men seated in front of her. They were discussing the possibility of leaping from the train at the next slowdown. They doubted it would make it to its destination, Breslau, and even so, they had no need to go there, they decided. It was too far to the east, they said, and overrun by the Soviets, so they studied a map in an attempt to find a shorter way to the west. Gretel did not intend to go to Breslau either. It was miles and miles out of the way, but neither could she jump off the moving train and start walking. There was no chance to get her bicycle out of the boxcar, and it would be useless now, anyway, so she waited, pondered her fate, and continued to gaze out the window.

The countryside looked peaceful and bright, with a full moon reflecting off the snow. The picturesque view made Gretel long for the winsome, moonlit, snowy evenings when she and Jakob would ride Baroque.

The train journeyed past a forest, which eventually opened into a large clearing. Gretel gasped when she noticed a road that ran along one side of the railroad tracks, which were elevated high above it. She witnessed hundreds of people traveling on the brutal, snow-packed road. Most were on foot, struggling just to stand. Some fell, and those who were too weak to get up again were destined to die; there was no room for them on the wagons. For one delusional moment, Gretel imagined she saw the little frozen boy sitting on one of those horse-drawn carts, waving.

Then, there was noise…so much noise it was deafening! They were under attack. The Red Army had been waiting for them in the clearing! There were the sounds of screaming, gasping, and bullets hitting the train; then, too, the pleas of people praying and the footsteps of those running down the aisle of the railroad car. These all melded into one evil sound.

Like sheep to the slaughter, Gretel followed the other passengers as they moved toward the doorways. She tried to open the door nearest her, but was unsuccessful, so she scuffled with her suitcase and the blanket until she made it to another one. Two soldiers jumped, but Gretel froze.

"*Sprung, Fraulein!*" someone behind her yelled, but she could not jump; she was too afraid.

"*Nein! Ich habe angst!*" she shrieked, her voice quivering. Yes, she was afraid, but so was everyone else, and the group took no pity on her. Someone pushed her, and she tumbled out, her belongings flailing about. Gretel ran for an underpass, but someone stepped on the blanket she was dragging, so she let it go. When she slid down a snowy embankment, she lost her prized little suitcase, too.

A fierce gunfire assault erupted, and the resulting reverberations came from every direction. It did not take Gretel long to distinguish the two types of screams she heard: those of unabashed fear and those of agonizing, unbearable pain. The night lit up with multicolored chains of ammunition fire. Some bullets whizzed past Gretel's head so closely she could feel them. She dove to the ground, and from her prone position, looked up to see other people running for an underpass. She got to her feet and followed them. Her lungs felt on fire, and she inwardly cursed her wobbly legs, willing them to go faster and faster, until she reached the underpass and leaned against a stone pillar, struggling for each breath.

"We have to try to get to that log house over there," someone said. Those who had dared to jump from the train fled toward this, their only refuge. Gretel followed suit. When one man stopped to vomit, a second man took his hand and lugged him along, still retching.

When she reached the cabin, Gretel fell to the floor like an empty sack. It was warmer in there, but crowded to the point of standing room only. No one spoke. All seemed to be holding their breath. There were no lights on in the cabin, but the moonlight shone through the windows, creating ghostly shadows on the strange assembly.

One woman began to shriek. Gretel slapped her, which snapped her out of her hysterical state, and whispered to the woman, "*Stoppen Sie das!*" The woman became silent, save occasional sobs that seemed more like hiccups. Another person, in a barely audible voice, reminded them that they must be quiet, lest they draw attention to themselves.

The gunfire ceased abruptly. Gretel and a few others inched closer to the windows to see what was happening. Soldiers were storming the train, slitting the throats of all who had stayed aboard, and dumping their bodies onto the ground like sacks of rotten potatoes. Some people broke free, but the soldiers caught up with them and began hitting them with the butts of their guns. When they fell, the victims met their fate with a bayonet through the stomach. Strange wisps of warm vapor rose from their disemboweled intestines, but when Gretel saw a Red soldier raping a dying teenager, she could no longer look. Literally hundreds of people died during that raid—men, women, and children alike. When they had finished with their macabre assault, the attackers disappeared into the woods, loaded with a variety of loot they had plundered from the dead.

In the moonlight, the soldiers could surely see the cabin where Gretel and the others were hiding, but they never checked it out. Why? In addition, those on the train could see the little shelter as plainly as those who took refuge in it could see them, so why did they stay on the train, seemingly awaiting such a fate? They did not even try to run. What godly or ungodly prerequisite was there that determined who would live and who would die? Gretel was not able to finish her thoughts. She fainted.

When she regained consciousness, a man who smelled of urine gave her his hand and helped her up. Most of the crowd focused on the engineer, who nursed a gash on his cheek.

"Look, I think I can get the engine running again if someone will help me repair the water hoses," he said.

A woman with an unabashed air of aristocracy about her said firmly, "Why should I worry if the train gets repaired or not? I refuse to board it and be a victim of the next attack."

"I know nothing about repairing trains," said one young man apologetically. "I would not be helpful."

"It will take just twenty minutes," said the engineer. His pleading eyes scanned the group for at least one volunteer, but there was none.

Even two of his own railroad employees abandoned him and set out on foot for the next depot. Gretel followed them, deliberately staying a few steps behind. They trudged along like that for about three to four kilometers, until a glint of light caught one man's attention. It was headlights! "In the ditch, you!" he shouted at Gretel, who stood flabbergasted and motionless, so he picked her up and threw her there. He secured her silence by lying close to her with one of his heavy boots just centimeters from her face.

The approaching silhouette turned into a military truck, just as they had feared. It moved closer, and still closer, until they could hear the sound of the driver changing gears as it climbed the hill, but it was not until it crested the knoll that the sorry three noticed it was a *German* truck! They jumped out from the trench, hollering and waving to gain attention. Purposely or not, the driver kept going, empty truck box and all.

Gretel fought back tears. She figured any sign of weakness that might slow her cohorts down was just cause for them to abandon her.

The trio slogged on along the snowy, icy road for hours. Gretel began to fall behind, but when the men stopped at a small deserted house, she caught up again. There were no words exchanged when Gretel stumbled in. Instead, the men quietly devoured some dry bread they had found. They did not offer to share it with her; neither did she ask. The bearded one, named Otis, she had learned, looked at Gretel contritely and then turned away. The other man, Alan, wiped his runny nose with his sleeve.

When Gretel ventured outdoors to scoop up a handful of snow, a farm dog of some type with brown shaggy fur surprised her. He looked in her direction but did not look her in the eye. He appeared fearful and confused. Most likely abandoned when his owners fled, he was simply looking for food, just as Gretel was. He slunk away, and Gretel wondered if he would survive. With his timid nature, he certainly would not be successful at swiping food from another animal. Would he become the victim of a dog roast? *No time for that now,* Gretel thought, and went back inside the house to tell the men of a plan she had thought up.

"I do not think I can go on much farther," she told them. "I know I am walking on blisters, I can feel them bleeding. Besides, I am too weak."

Alan suggested she take her boots off for a while.

"No, I will never get them back on, because my feet are too swollen. I will stay here. Maybe some trucker will stop and give me a ride. Go ahead without me."

It was Otis, now: "We are going to take you with us, even if we have to carry you."

"How kind of you! I did not know you cared! *Danke!*"

Alan laughed. "Are you naive or something? With a woman along, we have a better chance to get a ride. Don't you see? We mean you no harm, *Fraulein,* but neither are we interested in saving your ass!"

The once-stoic Gretel began crying. "You are not the first one to call me naive," she said, and then turned away to wipe her own runny nose on her own sleeve.

The trio set out on foot again and eventually flagged down a German military truck with a canvas-covered box. In it were several wounded soldiers. One, riddled with shrapnel, was bleeding profusely. Gretel checked his wounds and found he was missing a large part of his left buttock and most of his scrotum. She felt sorry for him, not for the fact he might die, but because he was alive and in excruciating pain. She whispered under her breath, "Please, God, let him die."

Suddenly, the adrenalin rush that had motivated Gretel to keep going left her. Every muscle in her body ached, and she entered into a mazy state of semiconsciousness. At the Glasgow railroad station, the driver of the military truck tried to rouse

Gretel. When he spoke, she could barely understand him. His words sounded hollow and distant.

"You traveled about forty kilometers tonight," he said. "I would guess about ten kilometers of it on foot." When this lofty man kissed Gretel on the cheek and said, "For a short, tiny thing, you sure are a feisty one!" it annoyed her.

"For a tall person, you sure are a rude one!" she quipped. "Why would *you* care about my survival, anyway?" He took no offense.

Things were fading in and out again, and Gretel fought to focus. "Where is everyone?"

"The wounded soldiers have been taken inside the building. Your companions left and asked me to wish you well." He continued his attempt to apprise her of all that happened, but her responses were whimpers and her comprehension dim. He stopped his chatter and got Gretel to her feet; then he gently took her by the elbow, but she collapsed, so he carried her into the train station.

She sat on a bench in the waiting area, where someone held a glass of beer under her nose. The man had a black hat—or was it black hair? Blurry vision made it hard for Gretel to tell. She took a few sips of the beer and thanked him, and then a soldier gave her two pieces of so-called "army chocolate," loaded with caffeine and sugar for an energy burst. It tasted good, but Gretel got sick. "You should not have given her beer!" a woman scolded, and then helped Gretel outside until her near-empty stomach quit cramping.

Soon Gretel came back inside, sat on the bench again, head in hands, and began to assess her situation. Because she had lost her small suitcase, she had no money to buy food or a train ticket, no ration cards, no identification of any kind. How would she ever get to Kassel without those? In just an iota of time, Gretel had joined the ranks of thousands of indigent wartime vagabonds.

A train arrived and everyone began scurrying for the door. Without warning, a man yanked Gretel to her feet, shouting, "*Gehen Dame!*" Go? Go where? She had no ticket! He prodded her along, nonetheless. The train's destination was unclear, but it could go only west or southwest, away from the advancing Red

Army, and that was all anyone cared about. No one asked for tickets on this trek to the unknown.

The train lumbered on for hours. As she slept, Gretel's dreams unleashed only pleasant memories of her childhood. It seemed her mind cordoned off everything else—including the war itself, leaving Jakob behind, and Crystel's disappearance—until she would be capable of dealing with it.

At daybreak, the pleasant dreams ended. The train had arrived in Dresden, in what was now mid-February. Just a few days earlier, one of the most horrendous bombing attacks of the war had pummeled Dresden. However, Gretel and others did not know this before their arrival.

The number of refugees and fleeing soldiers had doubled the city's population to more than a million people. When the enormous firestorms of flaming sulfur bombs hit Dresden, the loss of human life was catastrophic. In two days, at least 35,000 people died, but other estimates were well over 250,000. The fires had incinerated so many bodies that perhaps only the departed souls of those who perished would ever know the truth. The attack happened at a time when a virtual sea of humanity—possibly a million people, at least half of whom were German refugees and soldiers—had gathered there after fleeing the Red Army.

Gretel timidly disembarked from the train and set out to find a Red Cross building where she might get something to eat. As she rounded the corner of the blocks-wide railroad station, she noticed a stench, an odor she had never smelled before. The air was murky, hazy, and surreal; she could hear small explosions, barely audible over the din at the railroad station. The vile, overwhelming stench intensified. It was so horrific it overwhelmed her, and she covered her face with her scarf and moved on.

A woman who had followed Gretel became wide-eyed and dropped to her knees. "God have mercy!" she screamed.

Then Gretel saw it, too. Along the sidewalks were bodies and body parts piled up like cordwood and stacked two meters high. It was a sea of mutilated, torn carcasses, some burned, set with rigor mortis, and bloated. Other bodies had melted into a tacky goop that stuck to the sidewalks. "God have mercy!" the woman screamed again.

Gretel had resigned from the Lutheran Church years earlier, but a long-suppressed memory of the Nicene Creed surfaced, and she began to recite it.

"*We believe in one God, the Father, the Almighty, maker of heaven and earth, of all that is, seen and unseen…*" Her voice trailed off.

Walking gingerly among the piles of rubble and human remains, Gretel zigzagged her way to an area where she saw living people. City crews were loading the torn bodies onto horse-drawn lumber wagons. One worker kicked the remains of an arm and elbow off a stoop with his boot. Then he sat down, pulled down his mask, and began to sip from a small bottle. Addressing Gretel, he said, "Four kilometers of this. Thousands killed. It will take more than a week to put them away."

He appeared insensate, except for his right foot, which was tapping wildly. He pointed to the rubble of what once had been a water fountain, "There is a woman there. Dead like the rest. She is holding a little child's hand…that's all…the hand. I could not find the rest."

Gretel ran in a directionless manner until she was so exhausted she put her back against the wall of an office building and slid down to a seated position on the sidewalk. Next to her sat a German soldier in a daze; he was pale and trembling.

"Where are you coming from, and where are you going?" he asked.

"I worked in Poland…kindergarten teacher…I just arrived here on my way to Kassel. Is there a section of the city that is undamaged? A place where they might have a Red Cross station or a restaurant? I need to find some food, and then maybe I will stay for a day or two to recuperate."

"Woman! Leave! This city is not safe! It is dangerous from within here and without! Get out while you can! It is no vacation spot. Are you naive or something?"

"But I have not eaten in so long."

"I heard there is a train leaving soon. You best get aboard it."

"What about you? You should come, too."

He looked Gretel in the eye and did not look down as he pulled up his right pant leg. He was gritting his teeth now and grimacing in pain. More than half of the calf was gangrenous and oozed a black and green gooey substance.

"I was injured. Now the damn leg is rotting. I won't be going anywhere."

"Someone should get you to the Red Cross building or a hospital!"

"I was there two days ago. They turned me down, said they were short of antibiotics and anesthesia and that they had to save it for people who had a chance to live. The hospitals are so crowded and supplies so scarce...It's not their fault."

"Do you have family I could contact?"

"Yes, but I do not want them to know. I have tossed anything that could identify me. Better they think I died quickly on the battlefield. Get out of here! At least you have a chance."

As she scurried back to the train station, Gretel blinked away her many tears and saw what would be her salvation: a train leaving for Berlin! It had standing-room only, so most passengers stood with their fronts pressing against another person's backside. Short little Gretel elbowed a man in the crotch in order to squeeze her way through the doorway and get in. The muttering and angry protests of others on board stopped abruptly when the door closed and the mélange of refugees realized there was no safe egress from this cattle-car-like form of transportation.

The restrooms were packed with people, too, and almost impossible to reach. Those in distress had no choice but to use the doors and windows. Attempts to pass the children to the windows for relief were futile. They usually missed and soiled the person holding them. There was no sense of modesty. The stench from dirty clothes, urine, feces, and the inability to tend to the matters of menstruation was sickening.

At Cottbus, a number of people left the train, creating more room to move about. Gretel staggered when she walked, but managed to weave her way to a window where the Red Cross was serving soup. People were passing all types of containers to the windows to get some. In her state of confusion, Gretel stuck her hand out to receive her portion, but she held no cup or mug, not even something as crude as an empty lard can. A tall, broad-shouldered Red Cross assistant, wearing a white apron and a scarf with a Red Cross on it, looked sympathetic to her plight and was visibly pained when she looked into Gretel's eyes. All she could do was shake her head no, and then she cast down her eyes and turned away.

The train lugged on. Eventually, Gretel made her way to the restroom. It was there that she discovered a bullet hole in her coat and a dried bloodstain on the thigh of her long underwear. She pulled the fabric away from the skin, revealing a scrape where a bullet had grazed her. She had not even felt it.

Minutes later, she stood outside the restroom, rocking with the sway of the train and making conversation with a German soldier. "I cannot believe I didn't know about the bullet! For two days, I did not know!" She giggled.

The soldier grinned and winked at Gretel, then loudly pronounced they had an injured woman aboard the train. He told a young fellow seated next to them, "Get up, you ill-mannered poor excuse of a man! Give this fragile, severely wounded woman your seat!"

The soldier escorted Gretel to the vacated seat, where she began to have a fit of uncontrolled laughter. In her advanced state of exhaustion, any one of Gretel's emotions could burst free and out of control, sometimes inappropriately.

Gretel drifted into a faint again, but was jolted awake when someone put a cold, wet, greasy substance in her palm. "Here, honey, put the cold cream on your face. You will feel better," said an older woman with a Ukrainian accent. Gretel could see only a hazy image of her, but managed a weak, "*Danke.*"

When Gretel rubbed the cold cream on her face, she got some in her eye, and the woman handed her a fresh hanky. "What city are you headed to, *Fraulein?*" she asked.

"Where are we now?"

"Nearly to Berlin."

"Oh! From there, I am only a few hours from Kassel. My home! I am nearly home," Gretel said softly.

She closed her eyes again, and her mind journeyed back east to Poland. Thoughts of Jakob were foremost, but she wondered if all of the children she so dutifully cared for were alive. Surely not, but she could pretend so. What was Crystel's fate? Memories of Mamma and Papa filtered in, and she knew she could not bear it if they were not alive. Helmut was probably dead, of course. "Oh! No!" she wailed aloud, "Helmut!" She had not thought of her brother in weeks and wondered how she could have put him and his mysterious disappearance to the back of her mind.

At Berlin, there was to be only a thirty-minute wait before the next train west moved out, so Gretel hurried toward it, lest it leave without her. There was no time to find food or water, but Gretel no longer cared.

What concerned her more than the hunger was getting through the manned gate to board the train. She had no money for a ticket and no identification, so Gretel waited behind the ticket taker. When he was briefly distracted, she ducked under the bars and snuck past him. He grabbed her sleeve, but she pulled away. He could not leave his post, so he shouted for help; but Gretel kept running and managed to jump aboard and lock herself in the train's bathroom.

Surprisingly, no one looked for her there. The bathroom was nothing but a smelly little stall with a stool. At best, two people might be able stand shoulder to shoulder while another sat on the commode, but Gretel stayed there in the filthy, tiny refuge, until the train began to move.

At Magdeburg, there was an hour delay entering the depot due to some bombing in the area. The passengers were restless and their moods testy. Eventually, the engineer decided to reroute the train, and three hours later it arrived in Kassel.

The long, dark night had ended, giving way to a beautiful sunrise, and from the window, Gretel could see the statue of Hercules high upon the mountain, where it overlooked the city. She smiled, and then took a deep, long, nervous breath. Her parched mouth was agape and her heart raced wildly with anticipation. She was "home" now, that much was true, but what would she find there?

CHAPTER 8

While Gretel waited to get off the train, an SS officer came aboard. He was validating tickets and papers. His stern, militaristic air terrified her even more than being under gunfire. She stuck her fist in her pocket to retrieve the handkerchief the woman had given her for removing the cold cream from her face. With trembling hands, she swiped it on her dirty coat and rubbed her face with it, then mussed her hair, which she had just finger-combed minutes earlier. Perhaps if he saw her even more disheveled than she already was, and she showed him the blood stains from her wounds, he would believe her story.

Gretel had hurled her Red Cross band onto a tree branch after delivering the baby, so she would not be expected to do that again or to care for the wounded. The SS would deem such actions inexcusable, even though she was in survival mode and could not delay her passage back to Germany any longer. Had they found out? Did they know more? Her thoughts ran rampant. Did the SS know about Jakob? Was the SS on the lookout for her? She had evaded a ticket master to board a train without paying. Would they jail her?

"Oh, sir!" she said when he approached her. "I am so glad to see Kassel and members of our esteemed SS too! You see, sir, I have had the worst possible trip here from Poland, where I, too, served the party. I was a well-respected kindergarten director," Gretel babbled on. "We were under fire…I had to walk…I lost my papers, too!"

"*Fraulein! Sie liegent!*"

"No, sir! I do not lie!" She glanced around and saw that other passengers were getting impatient. When she unbuttoned her coat to show him the bullet hole in it, he could see her emaciated state. Gretel kept her composure, but when the officer scowled at her, she shouted for all to hear: "Shoot me if you must! I do not care anymore! I have had all I can take!"

To her amazement, he patted her on the head. "Poor thing, it looks like you need to get home fast," he said. Then he asked for her parents' name and address, wrote it down, and told Gretel to present the paper when she went through the gate at the station. "*Gehen Sie!*" he said, granting her permission to leave.

"*Danke,*" was all Gretel could manage to say.

When he left, other passengers started to question and chide her: "What did he want of you?" "See how you delayed us!" Gretel took refuge in the restroom until all other commuters had departed. She bawled uncontrollably, but more from relief than any other reason.

* * *

Kassel was quiet…too quiet. A heavy blanket of snow covered the ruins of the city the way a sheet covers a corpse. A few tall buildings were black and windowless. This made them appear to have dark rectangular eyes that stared out at the gray sky in distress, standing amid heaps of rubble on all sides from other structures now collapsed.

Surprisingly, a streetcar still ran, and Gretel rode it two kilometers until it came to the Fulga River, where it stopped because the bridge was gone. Gretel walked along the riverbanks to the skeleton of what had been a glorious, awe-inspiring church. Despite her excruciating pain, Gretel managed to climb the first six steps leading to the sanctuary door. From there she overlooked the burned-out remains of castles once owned by Hessian princes and the heap of rock that had been a beautiful opera house. She rested a few minutes, and then shuffled on to find her family.

Gretel reached the apartment building her grandfather had left to her in his will and was visibly shaken at the sight of what was now a bombed-out hull.

She lost all sense of time as she continued to follow the river bend to where she could see her parents' home, or what was left of it. Two women dressed in black coats, black stockings, and black shoes picked through the debris like ravens through garbage. Gretel remembered her great-grandmother's silver. How often and how lovingly her mother had polished it! Surely it had vanished days or weeks ago, and that hurt her more than the loss of the apartment building.

She was sad for the lost belongings, but gritting her teeth and enduring the pain of her bloody feet, she plodded on to find her parents. "They are alive!" she shouted aloud, forbidding herself to think otherwise; but even so, how would she find them? When she began to hyperventilate, Gretel removed her gloves and though her hands were numb with cold, cupped them over her mouth until she regained her composure.

The horrific sights surrounding her did not stop Gretel's warm reminiscences of her childhood and her parents. Her memories came one after another, as if escaping from a genie's bottle: a rapid succession of pleasant thoughts, such as taking her father's lunch to his office each day.

In a stark revelation, she realized where she might look for him. "Father! Father!" she screamed. She would look for him in his office!

Gretel ran a few steps, then fell, scooped herself up again, ran again, fell again, repeating this process for two blocks, her bloody feet pulsing with pain. Hysterical blindness took over, her vision fading in and out. She collided with someone and blurted out "*Excusez-moi*" in French, her mother's first language, and so Gretel's too. Surprisingly, a woman's voice responded, "*Mon Dieu!*" (My God!) She offered to help Gretel, but Gretel pushed her away and stumbled on until she reached the region's administrative building, which had suffered minimal damage.

She made it to the foyer, but could not reach the stairs to her father's office. She crumpled to the floor in a heap of human devastation. Gretel began screaming like a banshee, her voice echoing in the empty lobby, hoping her father could hear her pleas from his office.

"Papa! Papa!" she shouted.

"I am here, Gretel!" he answered and ran to her.

They sat on the floor together, her head on his chest, for what seemed a very long time. "Mamma will want to see you!" he said and carried Gretel a short distance to an unfamiliar apartment building.

Her parents had rented two rooms of a six-room apartment, and were living with three other adults and a child, all of whom shared a single bathroom. The building had no running water, which meant they had to carry water the distance of a ten-minute walk. Gretel's parents had been able to rescue some of their furniture, including the bedroom set, which made things more comfortable in their small refuge.

"Mamma! I have missed you so much!" Gretel said when she saw her, but Mamma was withdrawn and looked old. She hugged Gretel briefly, pulled back at the sight and the odor of her, and began to make the usual polite introductions to the others who lived there.

"She's not herself," Papa whispered.

Her mother looked away while Papa cut her boots off. He gasped when he saw that her engorged feet were oozing pus and blood. Some of the blood was black and coagulated, while some blood was fresh, and the surface layer of skin had fallen off in places.

Mamma got a warm pan of water for Gretel to soak her feet in, and a woman named Elizabeth got her a nightgown and some things for a sponge bath. All the while Gretel eyed a pot of potatoes boiling on the stove.

Mamma drained the potatoes, about seven of them, and put them in a bowl on the table. Gretel ate them slowly, one by one, but when Papa suggested she slow down, she realized she had eaten most of their week's ration in one sitting, and they had not had the heart to stop her.

A somber evening followed. Gretel and her parents discussed the fate of people they knew, detailing which ones were alive and which were dead. They spoke of friends and family whose fate was unknown, including Helmut.

"In a way, I am glad to hear that no one knows his whereabouts," Gretel sighed. "At least there is hope he is alive." When she nodded off, she would have fallen forward from her seat except that Papa caught her. He laid her on the small couch they'd managed to save and covered her. "*Schlaf gut,*" he whispered.

Through the night, sirens screamed as warplanes flew overhead, but Gretel never heard them. Her mother and father tried, but could not wake her to go to the bomb shelter, so they stayed with her all night.

Gretel slept each night on a small couch in one of the two rooms that had become her mother and father's home, until, after a few days, a painful but necessary blow came.

"You have to move out," Papa told her. "We pay a small rent here, but nevertheless we are guests. Elizabeth, especially, finds this crowded situation unbearable, and they do not want still another person living here."

"We know of a place nearby that has one very small room," Mamma added. "They know of your terrible trip and of your financial situation, so they are willing to let you have it free of charge for one week. Then you must pay rent."

"I understand, Mamma, but first I want to show you and Father something." Gretel pulled Jakob's ring from her pocket. "I am engaged to a Polish man. I met him when he did some electrical work for the school."

"You referred to him in your letters, but I had no idea it had come to this," Mamma said.

"I will not mention him again, because I do not want you to fear what people would say. If there is anything more you should know, I will tell you first. Right now, I don't even know if he is alive," Gretel said, surprised at how devoid of emotion she sounded.

"*Mein lieb*," Gretel's mother said. "You have changed, your taste in men, too." She smiled now and stroked her daughter's hair. "Perhaps he has been a good influence, though. You do not twist your hair anymore. *Ja?*"

"Actually, Jakob never mentioned it, but I am a changed person, and so are you. Do you know why, Mamma? Just as bombs destroy buildings, war disintegrates the person we once were. We are forced to rebuild our lives, but we will never be the same."

Mamma began to cry, so Papa flashed Gretel a disapproving look and quickly changed the subject. "Come, Gretel, we must not dwell on the war. I will show you the place you will stay."

Gretel moved into the small room, but it held no future for her and felt very much like a coffin. Air-raid sirens sounded day and night. The planes made two distinct sounds: one when they were about to drop bombs on Kassel, and another, heavier, sound when they were loaded with ammunition and on their way to another location. The sound of the airplanes and the wailing of sirens became so common that Gretel did not always head for shelter.

On one particular night when the raids were heavier than usual, Gretel did run for a bunker a block away, where she sat for hours with her parents and neighbors. They could not hear the bombs falling while in this four-level cement and steel cage—constructed so two stories were above and two stories were below ground—but they knew each time the bunker had been hit because of the way the room swayed and then stood still again. A few flecks of cement chips that had fallen to the floor were the only visible damage.

When Gretel returned to her room, she saw that the only window in it was shattered and a large piece of metal as sharp as a razor had sliced open her pillow. Feathers drifted about the room, reminding her of Adel and the mess he made when he butchered and plucked chickens. She cried for him, for little Thomas, for Crystel and Jakob, and for the life in Poland that was, and would never be again. *Gretel! Ich finde Sie!* were the words Jakob carved into the door, but how? When would he find her?

Gretel beat the butchered pillow and wailed in agony. Tears drenched her cheeks, but she did not dry them; she simply caught the salty droplets with her tongue. When one lone feather stuck to her quivering lip, she spat it on the floor and cursed the war, again.

Gretel moved a dresser in front of the window, cleaned up the glass, metal shards, and feathers, and then attempted to get some sleep. The air bombs had done their dirty work for the night, and in the morning, she would help with the daily search for the dead and dying. There would be corpses on the streets to remove, and cadavers from homes and basements to dispose of.

Some of the dead appeared to have no injuries save a small amount of blood on their lips, because they died when the air bombs burst their lungs. These bombs hit with a force so strong they sent heavy objects, such as ice chests, flying through the air like strange deadly missiles.

Gretel spotted the body of Hanna, one of her mother's closest friends, lying on the sidewalk, and stepped in front of Mamma so she would not see it, but without success. Mamma saw that a bomb had torn Hanna's skirt off, leaving her behind exposed, so she quietly took the coat off a dead man nearby and covered Hanna for modesty's sake.

"Mamma, I am so sorry," Gretel said.

"Stupid woman drank all my best tea when she visited," her mother muttered, then walked on.

It seemed everyone in Kassel was enveloped in despair, without even the most modest of necessities, and no work was available for Gretel to help pay her way, so she moved in with an aunt who lived in the country about sixty kilometers away. She had stored some of her clothes there before she went to Poland, and now she needed them badly.

Low-flying warplanes, mainly the British "Spitfires," wreaked havoc along the train routes in the countryside, but the small farming communities did not come under attack as often, so she felt safe there. Nevertheless, over the next few weeks Gretel became bored, so she contacted the Social Welfare Office about finding work. The party boss assigned Gretel to a teaching job in Beroun, Sudetenland, an annexed part of Czechoslovakia, but she had no idea the Allies had advanced well into that country and were moving west.

German military officials concealed any bad news from the media, and if the press did get wind of any negative information, they kept silent, fearing the consequences of releasing it. Besides, the party would never admit to the press that the German army was being defeated.

For the German population in general, there was little outside information to glean by listening to the *Voice of America*, then called *Soldiers' Broadcast West*. The broadcast was either jammed or ineffective, and few Germans dared listen to it.

German intelligence insisted that the Reds had halted their march through Poland and that the German army was forcing them back into Russia. The Hitler regime also claimed that the Allies would not get past the Siegfried line in France; therefore, the defeat of the enemy was certain, and the "Great Wonder Weapon" was near completion. Thus, many everyday Germans, disconnected from the truth, did not know otherwise.

However, Gretel knew by now that anything the Nazis said was in their best interest, and a bare pittance of their rhetoric was the truth. In light of this, she knew others might think it nonsensical for her to go to another occupied country. Perhaps it was her naiveté or some state of denial about the danger in Czechoslovakia that made her unafraid, but she longed to be somewhere she would not be a burden and somewhere she could earn some money. For that reason, on April 1, 1945, with all her official papers now replaced, Gretel said goodbye to Kassel again, and embarked on another journey by train to her new job, assuming the war would be over in weeks.

She was to see the party boss in Prague, about 450 kilometers from Kassel, to receive her official dispatch to Beroun. Gretel knew it would be a long trip, considering the poor connections, delays, rerouting, and unscheduled stops common at the time. In addition, the railways were bombed frequently, so people never knew what to expect from one stop to the next. But at least this time connections to Erfurt-Thüringen went smoothly.

The train was only a few kilometers from Erfurt when British Spitfire planes attacked, so the engineer sounded one fearsome, long whistle blast that warned, "Take cover!" In less than a minute, the train was vacant. People crawled under the coaches, threw themselves into ditches alongside the tracks, hid anywhere out of sight. Gretel hesitated, unsure what to do, until she saw the familiar silvery "flying dragons" drop down from the blue sky, assailing anything and anyone below. She scurried to a cement culvert, dropped to her hands and knees, and stuck her head inside it, leaving her posterior exposed. "Better my behind than my head sticking out," she muttered, but when she attempted to wriggle in a little further, she heard a male voice roaring with laughter.

"That's as far as you go! This half of the tunnel is mine," a German soldier said.

"That's not very chivalrous. Ladies first!" Gretel chuckled.

The two strangers lay nose to nose in this dark, clammy confine, rollicking with amusement while in the midst of danger. Bullets rattled against the trains, but Gretel and the soldier continued to converse as if they had just met somewhere in a coffee shop.

"I recently had a leg patched up, and now I'm returning to the front. I hope my leg will hold out. The Reds are moving pretty fast these days," the man said.

"Where is the eastern front now?" Gretel asked.

"Some area of Poland, I'm told. I am not sure where it has moved since I left there to recuperate from my injury. I'll find out when I get further orders, but I tell you the truth, *Fraulein*, I would rather be there than in the big German cities right now."

The planes left as quickly as they had come, and at the sound of three short whistle blasts, everyone hurried back to the train. Ten minutes later the train stopped at the depot in Erfurt, where Gretel needed to switch trains. Since no trains would be leaving until morning, she spent the night in an overcrowded waiting room, where it took an hour just to buy a couple of sandwiches.

The next day the train to Leipzig rolled uninterrupted through beautiful countryside where farmers were planting their fields. Spring had arrived in its regal beauty, and it might have been easy for Gretel to forget the ugliness of war, except for the views of devastated cities and towns alternating with the beautiful mountains and lakes.

A stop at Leipzig proved to be disheartening. It had not received as much damage as Dresden, but this formerly beautiful city was just another on the list of those left scarred and broken. Gretel felt uneasy there, and during the six-hour delay she paced furiously.

Back on board the train, she relaxed, settled in, and exchanged niceties with the passenger seated next to her. Neither one of them spoke of the war, but Gretel grinned wryly when she read a sign on the wall that read, "*Roder nussen rollen fur den Sieg, unnute Reisen verlanger den kreig.*" (Wheels must roll for victory. Needless trips will lengthen the war.) Someone had replaced the word for *wheel* with the German word for *heads.* The mood for Gretel and many other Germans had turned from prideful to sarcastic, with a heavy dose of bitter pessimism, and there was a clear sense of defeat in the air.

Gretel recalled her father saying, that after World War I, Germany had had to choose between Communism and Nazism, and it chose what it felt was the lesser of two evils. But now it faced a potentially much worse fate. She could only wonder if Hitler was correct with his oft-repeated words: "Germany must win the war, even if it resembles a plowed field to do it!" and "Victory or death!" Gretel continued her musing, but she could never speak publicly about her misgivings concerning the war and Hitler. She would head on to Sudetenland and possibly a better future.

Sudetenland was an annexed area of Czechoslovakia that had been under German control for most of the previous twenty years. The Germans and Czechs living there had tolerated each other until recently, but now the Czechs showed their hostility openly, and the Germans had their misgivings as well. Gretel had been warned of this, but however unfriendly the environment, she decided it would be preferable to being in the German cities with the ongoing destruction and death and the bombings. She continued on to Czechoslovakia.

CHAPTER 9

In Prague, the party chief futzed through Gretel's papers, muttered that he had received little information from the upper echelon about her duties, and then instructed her to contact the county nurse when she reached Beroun.

Gretel could not keep her eyes off him. There were scars on the right side of his face, conceivably from a previous burn, and only one eye moved when he looked at her. He was pale, thin, and feeble looking, and his uniform too large and wrinkled. Most unattractive were his nose hairs, long and protruding like corn silk from his unusually big nose.

"It seems, Fraulein Sennhenn, you will be in charge of thirty children ages six to ten; that is all these documents say."

"Why are they not in regular school?" she asked. "School resumed on April first, and they would not be on a holiday. What, exactly, are my directives once I get there?"

"I told you to see the county nurse! I am busy! Do not question me further!"

Gretel's previous experiences with the SS had convinced her that she should say what these men wanted to hear and not argue with them, so she made her eyes downcast and displayed a humble expression on her face. "*Ja offensichtlich,*" she said softly. "*Sind se korreckt.*"

He ignored her apology, as well as an opportunity to give her a lecture extolling his authority. His demeanor was not haughty and self-important, the way most of the party bosses presented themselves. In fact, there was no ostentatious air about this man at all. He was not the usual by-the-book authoritarian figure the Nazi leaders normally portrayed. After putting some keys in his desk drawer, he mumbled a subdued "Heil Hitler," absent a salute, and exited the room quietly, leaving Gretel no chance to ask for advance pay. This high-ranking Nazi official's behavior of disrespect toward the Reich revealed that to him Hitler was no longer sacrosanct and that he was not alone in his opinion.

When she arrived in Beroun, Gretel asked people there for directions to the school, but received only cross looks and no answers. Gretel knew very little Czech, and the indignant population, annoyed by the German occupation, refused to speak German to her, although most had learned both languages in school. She took their cue, said nothing more, and began to walk in the direction one man had pointed.

Some of the buildings wore the pocks of age, and it was obvious they needed repair, but to Gretel, the architecture was charming. It was a gorgeous spring day, and the flowers were so beautiful that Gretel did not hurry. A few blocks later, she paused briefly when the smell of just-baked bread enticed her; but its tantalizing smell came from a home, not a bakery, so she moved on. Her empty stomach audibly protested.

Eventually, Gretel found the address, a disheveled old building that had once been a schoolhouse. When she knocked, no one answered, so she timidly opened the door. The room was crowded, dirty, and the noise inside was deafening. Small wonder no one had heard her rapping.

When Gretel introduced herself as the new teacher, a puffy-eyed woman with a filthy green dress and an equally dirty apron said, "Fraulein Sennhenn, I am Frau Henning, call me Olga. In case no one told you, this is now a detention camp. Well, I am in charge here, and please know that we welcome your help. There are two hundred German citizens living here. We are but a few of many surviving evacuees from the area around Breslau, Poland, forced to leave months ago, long before the Russian break-through. We feel in limbo, and we are not happy about living in still another occupied country, but what are we to do?"

Gretel watched in awe while children ran about undisci-plined, babies cried, and mothers argued with each other. The sorry group had only straw mats covered with dirty sheets to sleep on.

Olga complained to Gretel that the horses the displaced Germans owned, now boarded at various farms on the edge of town, were living in better conditions than their owners were.

"Well, Gretel—I assume I may call you Gretel—dig in and help wherever you are needed."

Gretel stood voiceless with a perplexed expression. Had she misunderstood? This was supposed to be a teaching position! Just then, a wet diaper whizzed past her head, but Gretel saw it com-ing, ducked, and put her forearm over her eyes.

"Frau Hein!" Olga screamed, "that's enough!"

"That lazy sloth Bertina Walter borrows my son's diapers and does not even wash them properly before she returns them! She has not even the courtesy to hang them out to dry!" Frau Hein complained.

"And you can do better?" Frau Walter said. "I scrubbed them until I had bloody sores on my knuckles from the washboard! There is no decent soap to wash them with, not enough hot water, and there was no room on the clothesline to hang them; so what am I to do? I will not borrow your diapers again. Instead, I will cut up one of your dresses! I would have enough fabric for twenty diapers!"

"*Stoppen Sie das!*" Olga demanded. "You two settle this, or you can haul water the rest of the week!"

A young teenager with old eyes and sunken cheeks motioned to Olga that the slop pails needed emptying. Olga patted her on the shoulder. "Yes, dear, that would be helpful. Take a couple of the boys with you."

She turned to Gretel. "Emma can hear and understand, but she cannot speak. The girl is in shock since her mother and two siblings died in a dreadful wagon accident on the way here. It rolled into an icy cold river, they were pinned under it, and she watched them drown. Her father survived, but died of complications later. I made her my assistant. You will have no problem communicating with her."

"Speaking of communicating," Gretel said, "I know French and Italian, but I never learned to speak Czech. Are you able to converse with the Czechoslovakians, Olga?"

"Yes. I was born in Germany, in Dusseldorf. I am a German national, but my grandparents are Czechoslovakian, so I speak both languages, and the county nurse does too."

"Where is she?"

"She is at her house."

Olga's eyes directed Gretel toward a window where she could see a building that used to be the schoolteacher's house. Its outhouse, made of old, splintered wood planks, was an abhorrent, nasty gray; however, the house itself, both its brick exterior and the roof, remained in good shape. Gretel could tell the building was tiny—three rooms at best—and once had what looked like a huge vegetable garden, though it now was full of last season's dead weeds. Even so, the fruit trees were prolific with new buds, their tiny fertile embryos waiting to burst forth with new life.

After Olga showed Gretel where to put her suitcase and handbag, she escorted her to the little house to meet the nurse, Gertrude, an extremely tall woman with straight gray hair pulled back in a low ponytail. She was busy cutting up old fabric for bandages. She did not stand to greet Gretel and did not look her in the eyes. At once, a sizable schism developed between the two.

"So, the party sends us a kindergarten teacher. I need another nurse! Fraulein Sennhenn, these kids are not able to learn under such conditions, because half of them are sick. If they are to learn anything, they must get well first."

"*Ja*, I understand that. I do have some nursing training, and I learned a lot when I was in Poland. I was head kindergarten director at a sizable school where we had an excellent nurse, who taught me so much..."

"Then put your knowledge to work, *Fraulein*. You will just have to fill two roles. Most every one of these children has lice, impetigo, or scabies; you can start there, but your first priority is caring for the people in the infirmary. Adults here have needs, not just the children. I will show you where our little hospice room is."

Gretel had to move quickly to keep up with Gertrude's long-legged stride back to the school-turned-refugee camp. There they came to a door with a Red Cross symbol on it. Inside were eight beds,where babies were born next to dying old folk. The beds were army cots with straw mattresses, straw pillows, and a meager supply of stained, thin old sheets and moth-eaten blankets. The sun shone through the window, highlighting a bloodstain on the floor, and flies hovered over a commode someone had emptied, but not rinsed.

Gertrude had told the truth. The people in this infirmary needed extensive care, and some were at death's door. It was not a place for someone with a simple head cold or stomachache, as the infirmary at the Wolfsbergen Kindergarten was.

"The doctor comes on Tuesdays and Fridays to bring supplies, give me advice, and have the sickest ones transported to the hospital," Gertrude explained. "Obviously, we call him for emergencies, too, but I warn you, he is a strange one! He takes too much time examining the little boys, if you know what I mean, so I would not leave him alone with them. But he is sympathetic to our plight and uncomplaining. Even so, you will call him only at my discretion. Is that clear?"

Gretel turned her head away as tears welled in her eyes. How had this happened? She, the once-respected Kindergarten Director Sennhenn, resented being a servant to this woman. She despised this disheveled abode with its unsanitary conditions, and pined for the neat, orderly school she had so effectively organized.

The women bickered over frequently revised schedules that were impossible to keep, the lack of supplies that forced them to improvise, and who should assume which duties, but in time, the friction between Gertrude and Gretel lessened. They made peace with the conditions of war and with each other. They came to accept the fact that nothing could operate normally under such conditions, and they stopped trying. In addition, the camp leaders, such as Olga, held no certain authority here, so there was none to usurp and no discord surrounding it. And so Gretel, Olga, and Gertrude were able to cooperate and make the best of the situation.

For a few hours each day, Gretel took the older children to a tavern in town and attempted to teach them something, but her efforts were to no avail. On one afternoon when the children were unusually restless, she gathered them up and occupied them with a walk in the woods. She had intended to give them a lesson on the flora and fauna of the area, but British Spitfire fighter planes swooped down in a deliberate, taunting, childlike display of harassment. From that day on, she did not leave the refugee camp with the children.

The animosity between the Germans and the Czechs continued to grow. Soon, the town officials would no longer guarantee the safety of the refugees if they moved about town unsupervised, so most of them did not leave the school. Only Gretel and Olga left the schoolyard, and then only to buy necessary goods, such as food.

Soup and stew (there was never anything else) were prepared in a field kitchen dubbed the "goulash cannon." People argued about routine chores, and they fought over food, forcing Olga to lock up all foodstuffs between meals.

One evening, during the never-ending dishwashing and kitchen cleanup, a bomb hit a factory across the road. It was evidence that although the number of battles in that area had waxed and waned during the last several months, the war, in the broad sense, was as intense and brutal as ever.

On the last day of April 1945, while buying provisions at a local food market, Gretel and Olga overheard some Czechs talking about "liberation." These locals wore smug grins, and the undertone of their conversation seemed to be celebratory. Gretel tapped Olga on the shoulder, her eyes pleading to understand the scuttlebutt.

"They say the Allies are closer," Olga whispered.

Gretel's hands began to shake as they loaded the groceries onto a hand-pulled cart. The two made nervous conversation in low voices during the twenty-minute walk back to the compound, where a dozen of the refugees, many with panicky expressions, met them on the steps.

"What took you?" they shouted.

"What do you mean?" Olga said in a noticeably trembling voice.

"The nurse…Gertrude…she left in a hurry! What is going on? What are we to do?" they questioned.

"She probably was trying to catch up with us, in order to help with the groceries," Gretel reasoned. She smiled, though the terror within her was substantial.

"No!" someone insisted. "She had packed her things beforehand, and when you left, she did, and without a word."

"Someone picked her up in a car. I saw it!" a young boy said.

Olga pulled Gretel aside. "Gertrude knew! She knew something that we do not! The Allies *must* be coming, and she headed for the border!"

"More than once I saw her buy a pack of cigarettes and slip them into her coat pocket, but I never saw her smoke one. I am sure now that she was bribing someone," Gretel added.

Olga spat on the ground in disgust.

Gertrude's disappearance left Gretel and Olga to care for two small children with scarlet fever, an old woman near death, and a pregnant woman with complications. Olga called the office in Prague for help, but there was no answer.

"So, what are we to do now?" Gretel asked Olga.

"Gertrude ran scared. There is obvious danger. We will have to stay here until we know more. If it is not entirely safe for even one or two Germans to move about town, even to get needed supplies, then we as a group are all in peril. We must not draw attention to ourselves by attempting to leave en masse. We will have to make a plan," Olga said, and Gretel agreed.

"Perhaps the chattering we heard about the troops advancing was just rumors," they told each other, and continued with their work.

Olga called the doctor about the pregnant woman with complications. He expressed annoyance that she had been in the same house with scarlet fever patients, but he kept his word and sent someone to bring her to the hospital. The woman left behind her ten children, ages two to fifteen, their four suitcases, and a baby buggy. In addition to everything else, Gretel and Olga would now also be responsible for these children.

Without Gertrude, Gretel took over as the one who stayed in a separate room with the scarlet fever children. Their mothers or siblings dared not be around them, and, Gretel had experience with the disease. For the rest of the day, she worked tirelessly to care for these sick ones, while Olga handled the rest.

That evening at twilight, Gretel saw a strange sight from the isolation room. Four Czech guards with guns had posted themselves directly in front of the schoolhouse!

Gretel gasped when she heard a noise at the hospice door, but it was Olga opening the door just wide enough to slip in some food for Gretel. Gretel peeked through the small opening and told Olga about the eerie sight of the guards.

Olga's skin turned a grayish, sallow color, her eyes opened wide, and her pupils dilated. In a breathy, depleted voice, she whispered, "Oh God! We are finished, Gretel! They will lock us up, or worse! I should not be surprised to see the building go up in flames!"

Olga broke quarantine and came into the room to look out the window and see for herself. Three other soldiers were coming double-time now, up the walk toward the front door of the schoolhouse.

Olga screamed for people to lock the doors and close the windows, but almost simultaneously, the men were tramping up the stairs. Olga warily opened the front door, explained in Czechoslovakian that there was scarlet fever in the house. The bullies backed up in a hurry, but not until they forbade the women to speak German at the risk of execution.

The next day, May Day, was not cause for celebration. Except for a few people who broke down emotionally, that day and the following few days were uncomfortable, but uneventful.

The men continued to stand guard, permitting only Olga to go outside, with an escort, to get water or wood for the stove. But she could not bring enough of either for the hapless group; it was not a one-person job. The basement floor became their toilet, because the soldiers did not allow the refugees access to the outhouse. The situation was unbearable, and the guards showed no mercy. At least when an old man died, they did remove his body.

On May fifth, Gretel awoke to an overwhelming sight: outside the building was an American flag flying high above the Czechoslovakian one. A few hours later, someone replaced the U.S. flag with the Soviet flag. A fearful, paralyzing mood overcame the German captives.

When the guards barged their way in and began wrapping the children with scarlet fever in blankets, no one spoke, not even the children. Since the women feared the consequences of speaking German, Gretel used pantomime to ask Olga what the Czech soldiers were saying to her. Olga responded with gestures, indicating the guards told her they were transporting the children to a hospital. But Gretel saw no vehicle there. Without any further explanation, the men whisked the children, just three and five years old, away to an unknown fate.

The soldiers were hung over from drinking the night before and were ill-tempered, but they took pleasure now in commanding the Germans to get ready to leave. First, the men ordered them to pack their bags and sweep the floors. Then, when everyone was ready to go, they demanded that people take their bags outdoors where Gretel expected to find wagons and horses—but there were none. The men told Gretel and the other Germans to line up and get a good view while they stacked most of their suitcases in a pile, poured fuel on them, and set them ablaze. Gretel had kept her largest suitcase with her, as well as her purse, but poor Olga had only her purse and Gretel's medicine bag.

Gretel and Olga were glad to see that someone had corralled the ten children the pregnant woman had left behind, as well as the buggy, which held the two youngest. Likely, it was the young, mute Emma, so kind and helpful, who had done so. But when they looked around for Emma, they did not see her; they did notice that the thinnest of the Czech guards had slipped away. Gretel did not wonder what happened to Emma, she knew. "That poor girl," she whispered to Olga.

Now orders and verbal abuse came from everywhere, rapid fire, like bullets from guns: "Line up four in a row! We will escort you to the border! We are kind to do that much! We could shoot you all! We are expert marksmen, too!"

Gretel understood that the egotistical gloating of these soldiers only eclipsed the fear inside them. Without this process of denial, distancing themselves from the ineffable acts of war, those involved would not survive the emotional trauma resulting from what they had seen and done. Behind their outer shells, the military were as terrified as their captives; but each person—Axis or Allied, military man or civilian—did what it took to stay alive, and so would these soldiers. What was most terrifying, however, was the mob mentality, because it caused otherwise normal people to do evil, deliberate acts, and not only in self-defense.

The soldiers marched the group past the farmhouses to have one last look at their own wagons and horses, now displayed in the yards of those who had seized them. Local citizens lined the roads laughing and pointing.

"Your brown-uniformed German military mice have all deserted you or been stomped on!" one man shouted.

"The Allies have reduced your shitty-colored Nazi army to a stinking pile of diarrhea!" said another.

"For six long years we have lived under Nazi tyranny! No more!" said a woman holding a baby.

Their teasing and cavorting went on until every German was out of sight, but then more Czech guards and some other Allies arrived to taunt them. When they reached the highway, Red Army soldiers on motorcycles ran amok, roaring past them, pretending they would run them down. The slower people trekked on as best they could while being driven at gunpoint by soldiers strategically placed at the rear. The soldiers in the front slowed down the faster ones each time those in the rear fell behind, and in this way, they would regroup and stay in formation.

The displaced Germans had walked about two kilometers, when more than a dozen soldiers stopped them at a crossroad and ordered them to face the hillside. The men were pointing to a clearing, and all of the downtrodden Germans looked in that direction. Gretel blinked her disbelieving eyes when she saw a machine-gun nest, complete with muzzles, looking back at them!

Next, their attention turned to two severely injured German soldiers, abandoned by their forces and now dragged to the side of the road. One of the wounded was missing a leg and had been using a self-fashioned crutch. The other had lost an arm. The Allied soldiers bashed them repeatedly with the butts of their guns and pushed them into the ditch. A woman who had been traveling with the mortally wounded men began wailing and threw herself on top of one of them, possibly her son. Soon, she too received numerous blows to the head, and all three lay silent.

Then, an anonymous voice demanded Gretel and the rest to face the machine guns with their hands over their heads, and Olga could take it no more. She screamed like a banshee, dropped to her knees, and with her hands still over her head began shouting a fervent prayer. The men dragged her to the front of the line, where they cut her thick auburn hair very short with a knife and brutally boxed her in the face.

The other refugees stood with arms above their heads for another ten minutes, or so it seemed. All became silent. The only sound was the wind as it soughed through the trees. But the silence was soon shattered when the men, now amused, began shooting into the air in a deliberate attempt to terrorize their charges. The men on motorcycles surrounded them again, chasing them on the run along the road and through an easily penetrable forest until they arrived at the border. Having finished their hoodlum-like behavior, the soldiers left.

"At last, we are on German ground!" one man shouted, but oddly, no one else joined in his revelry.

Olga broke rank from the rest of the group, bolted away, and hid behind a downed tree. Gretel ran after her and found her sitting on the ground, sobbing, one eye already swollen shut. Blood trickled down her cheek, and the more she tried to wipe it away, the slimier her hands got. Gretel tried to help, but as demoralized as Olga was, she did not want Gretel near.

"*Gehen Sie weg!*" she yelled to Gretel.

"*Nein!*" Gretel shouted, insisting she would not leave. As she knelt to examine her friend's wounds, there was the distinct metallic smell of drying blood, combined with the odor of urine and human feces. Olga had messed her pants and began to whimper in embarrassment.

"I am so ashamed," she said between sobs.

"I will be right back, Olga, so stay here!"

Gretel ran to the roadside where she had left her suitcase, retrieved some white, thigh-length underwear, then scurried back to Olga. "Change into these," she said.

Olga would not look Gretel in the eye. "I'm sorry you had to see me in this state."

"I have cleaned up many a child and adult. So have you. This is nothing new to me. I caught the last train out of the region of Poland where I worked, and then I ended up on a train packed with refugees, like me. We were so crowded we stood crotch to ass. No one had a chance to relieve him or herself outside or at a toilet. It was the most disgusting smell! This is nothing. Do you want to hear something funny? One man who was pressed up against me got aroused!"

The last part of the story was not true, but it made Olga laugh, and she regained her composure.

Gretel treated Olga's wounds with items in her medical bag, and they returned to the road to join the others. In due time, some people said their farewells to the group and went other directions, heading toward their separate hometowns. For so long they had traveled, and still now the question of who would arrive at their destination safely and who would not would seem to be pure happenstance. Gretel made it clear that Olga would come with her to Kassel and recuperate before she moved on to Dusseldorf.

It was late in the afternoon, and what was left of the group had to find shelter for the night. Since arriving in Czechoslovakia, Gretel had been obediently wearing a Red Cross band, which in this case designated her as the leader.

"*Dieses ist nicht gut,*" Gretel confessed to Olga. "I do not know where to go or what to do. Anyone else could serve as well as me."

"If that is so, Gretel, do not tell the others that. If only you give them the *impression* you know what you are doing, they will not panic, and they will not give up. We cannot allow them to lose hope. They...we...have all been through too much."

Olga's grotesquely swollen lip made her words hard to understand, but Gretel knew she was right. She led the group along the same road they had been on, and in about an hour, they reached a village.

CHAPTER 10

When they spotted a small farm, complete with a welcoming barn, people wept openly and thanked God. It was a gorgeous, mild spring evening; even so, Gretel shivered with nervousness as she stepped forward, introduced herself, and explained to the small-framed older farmer what these people had experienced.

"*Willkommen! Willkommen!*" he shouted while motioning them all to come, and then he led them to the barn. He became concerned about the welfare of one little boy who had fallen and gashed his knee and of Olga with her battered body.

"I am Erik. You settle in, please, and I will get my wife, Mavis, to treat your injuries."

Mavis did not fit the image of the pudgy farm wife in a cotton dress and apron Gretel had so often seen. This woman was very gaunt and wore a flannel shirt over a woolen skirt.

Gretel was puzzled. Did the Nazis confiscate some of the food these people had produced in recent years? Was there no money to buy fabric for sewing clothes? Abruptly, Gretel regrouped her thoughts and began to focus on the here and now; there was no time for such pondering. Not now.

Mavis cleaned and wrapped the boy's injured knee, then directed Olga to the hand pump, where she could rinse her blood-soaked hair. Olga could not bend over to have her hair washed because the rush of blood to her bruised face made it throb, so six women leaned her back, then lifted her by the torso so she could tip her head back.

"I feel so silly!" Olga said and managed a faint chuckle.

When they were done washing Olga's hair, Mavis said, "I need to get something." She ran to the house, returned with some scissors, and trimmed Olga's chopped hair as best she could. Olga thanked her profusely.

"We can rinse your dress out, but I cannot do anything about the bloodstains, dear," Mavis said.

"I understand. May God bless you!"

In a gilded answer to the prayers of the grateful people, the farmer showed up with four large kettles of milk. Adults took less, for the children's sake, but all were able to partake. These members of the normally proud, clean, and orderly German race were now a dirty, smelly, and downtrodden assembly left to beg. Nevertheless, to immerse themselves in feelings of self-pity or humiliation was not an option. They just needed to sleep and move on again.

Many, including Gretel and Olga, climbed up to the hayloft, where not even the dust, itchy hay chaff, or the smell of bat guano bothered them. One by one, they drifted off into a deep and contented sleep.

In her dream state, Gretel felt the brush of Jakob's hand across her nipples. It stimulated her sexually, and she moaned in her sleep. An orgasm woke her, and she was both embarrassed and disappointed to realize what she had felt was just Olga's hand sweeping across her chest as she turned over in her sleep. Had it been Crystel lying there, Gretel would have giggled and confessed her excitement because they had freely shared even the most private things. Such was not the case with Olga, and Gretel lay pining for Crystel's perfect friendship; if Crystel were here, they would be stifling laughs, amused by the oddity of taking refuge in a barn with so many complete strangers.

To Gretel the smells of the barn were comforting; they reminded her of making love in the barn with Jakob and of the gentle horse Baroque. With the exception of a few mice scampering and people snoring, the barn had gone silent. Even the babies were still.

In her next dream, Gretel heard the sounds of wagons and horses. There she was again on the day she had left the kindegarten: cold, terrified, and escaping Poland. Jakob was running beside her wagon, holding a candle and shouting, "Gretel! *Ich finde Sie! Liebe dich!*" In this dream, he continued to profess his love, but someone cut the candlewick and she could see Jakob no more. All then went dark and silent, save the sound of wagons...

Gretel woke from her dream to someone gently tugging on her hair. "Gretel, wake up! Listen!" Olga whispered. "What is that noise?"

"I thought I was dreaming that!" Gretel told her. "It sounds like wagons, *loaded* wagons, pulled by horses! Is it more refugees?"

"I don't know. What should we do?"

"Olga, come help me."

Gretel and Olga climbed a ladder to the attic vent. They could hear more clearly now the steady grinding of wagon wheels. Gretel peered through the slats of the vent, then reached down to take Olga's sweaty, trembling hand and pull her farther up the ladder so she could see, too.

Although it was still dark, a short distance away on the main road they could make out a long trek of wagons, dozens of them pulled by horses; and from the sound, they were weighted down to capacity. It was all too curious.

Gretel did not sleep much the rest of the night. She lay quietly, with shallow, almost inaudible breathing, listening carefully and trying to comprehend what she could not see. The grinding of wheels went on continuously throughout the night.

When there was enough light for Gretel to see her hands, her fingers, and her dirty fingernails, she scrambled up the ladder to the vent again, and set eyes on a site that made her laugh uncontrollably. The rest of the people in the barn began to wake up, including Olga, who shook her head in amazement at what she saw.

The steady sound of trucks, grinding wagon wheels, and snorting horses came from Russian soldiers hauling the items they had looted from the Germans back home to Russia! The wagons held all sorts of household goods, even pianos and sewing machines. The soldiers had been working through the night, and the number of trucks and wagons must have been in the hundreds!

"Gretel! They can never get the stuff back to Russia in this way. What are they thinking?" Olga said.

"I don't know! Even if they could get the things to a freight train, it would take a week to load!"

At once, everyone in the barn woke and had to pee, so the procession began. A half dozen people lined up at the outhouse, but most of the men went behind the barn and turned their backs. The women took turns shielding one another from view while they relieved themselves. The ritual had become all too common.

The children were asking if they could have more milk, and Gretel told them it was too much to expect. But just then, Erik and Mavis arrived with more milk and four steaming kettles of potatoes! When they were finished, the refugees thanked their hosts profusely, paid them whatever they could manage for their hospitality, and moved on.

By noon, the group had dwindled to about thirty people as one by one, they had split off to journey to other locations, mainly east toward Breslau. Gretel, and the rest were traveling west.

One man shouted, "Good-bye, all! If we ever meet again, I will buy you a beer!"

"And I intend to get drunk with you!" Gretel chortled.

The next day it rained a steady spring shower that was cold but refreshing and cleansing. The children cried at first, but soon adjusted to it. Gretel and the other adults helped them find wild onions, dandelion greens, and other wild plants to eat along the trek, but a surprise was in store. Gretel spotted it first.

"Rachel! Olga! Distract the children," Gretel whispered. The women began running about wagging their tongues in the air to collect raindrops. The children laughed heartily and followed suit.

Soon, Gretel returned, holding something in her gathered skirt and sporting a wide grin. "Children, what can you guess that I have here?" she asked. "You must line up and each of you will get your share, but no pushing!" She then unveiled the surprise.

"Asparagus!" they shouted in unison. "*Danke*, Fraulein Sennhenn!"

"The youngest ones go first!"

"*Ja, Fraulein!*" they responded obediently.

Gretel showed the group where more of the asparagus was. It was an amazing patch of delicious greens!

"Thank the good Lord!" Olga said. "It will keep them going a little longer."

"We need to go now," Gretel said, sooner than some would have liked.

Unfortunately, such lighthearted moments traveled along with reality, and reality raced to the forefront once more. They struggled on, the ten orphans doing the best they could. The two oldest siblings had faithfully taken turns pushing the buggy with the two toddlers and the suitcase, even when one wheel fell off; but when a second wheel collapsed and the axle broke, they hoisted the youngest children onto their shoulders, lugged the suitcases along, and moved on.

Gretel whispered to Olga, "I am so proud of them, and they are so uncomplaining! It is early in the day and they will tire later. We will help them then, but for now, we will let them be. They are drawing strength by sticking together, and the older ones are doing a fine job caring for the small ones."

"You are the one trained in child development. I am not sure I agree, but all right."

Throughout the day, Gretel and her group met other groups of people ambling on to their individual destinations. They met soldiers, too: Nazi Germans, usually traveling alone or in pairs, who had fled Poland through Czechoslovakia. Enemy soldiers would ambush the German troops, fierce beatings would follow, and the victims of these marauders lay shoeless, dying, while their comrades abandoned them because they could not travel.

Occasionally, a soldier returning to Germany would notice Gretel's armband, stop her, and ask her to bandage various wounds. One time, a German lieutenant with several days' worth of beard growth pleaded for Gretel to give his friend, a captain according to his insignia, enough morphine to kill him.

The semiconscious soldier, beaten black and blue all over, had one eye missing and a deep gash across his head. His lower lip was gone and so was one fingernail. A rivulet of blood soaked his chest. He also had a broken arm and a compound fracture to his femur. His bare feet were bloody.

Gretel nudged Olga, and after a quick tilt of her head and a glance to her right, Olga understood. She would take the children to a field some meters away so they would not see the beaten-up soldier.

"Please, I will beg if I must, but give him enough morphine to kill. If I make it back, I will tell his family he died bravely and quickly in battle. They must not know the Czech guards tortured him. He is in agony. Please do something!"

"When he cries out, talk to him, and that will comfort him," Gretel said.

"He was with me when the enemy soldiers ambushed our unit. Those shot dead by the Russians were better off for it, because some Czechs made sport of torturing their captives, like my friend here. They behaved like schoolboys killing a bug!"

Gretel shuddered. "Oh, dear God! How did you get him here?"

"I carried him two kilometers to the border. We met some people with a wagon who gave us a ride to this place." He moved his hand around "They left us here when they were ready to turn off on that road, a very rough road. The man said my friend would not make it anyway, and that our weight in the wagon was tiring their horse."

"What did you do when you were attacked? How is it you, yourself, were not hurt?"

He vaulted toward Gretel, collapsed in her arms, and began to wail in distress. "Damn you, woman! I hid like a frightened child! That is what I did! I must help him die and then bury him. It is the least I can do."

Gretel's heart pounded as she weighed the idea of killing outright a man already in the throes of death with a fatal dose of morphine, versus giving him enough to take the edge off the pain.

"I am sorry about your friend," she said, as the soldier stroked the dying man's hair.

Without another word, Gretel knelt down, opened her medicine bag, and gave what was left of a fine soldier an injection of morphine.

"Tell his family he was a hero."

The man hugged Gretel tightly, and she did not cringe when his salty tears ran down her cheek.

By early afternoon, just three adults and the ten children the pregnant woman left behind trekked along with Gretel and Olga. It was then that they met up with several Russian soldiers sitting at the edge of the road and eating soup from a cast-iron kettle that hung over a fire.

"Come join us," they cajoled.

The men seemed friendly enough, but Gretel was edgy. What did these Red Army men want? Their gracious offer seemed suspicious, but she reminded herself not to fall victim to their chicanery. She began to babble to the soldiers.

"The children are so tired, and they have been whimpering. We would not want them to disturb your conversation. Given the chance, I think, we would eat all that is left, but we would not want to be so ill-mannered…we would never intrude…"

The Russians did not know enough German to follow her ramblings, but laughed heartily at it. They all held their breath while the men searched each person for loot such as watches and cameras, but there was very little to procure. They stole several things, including someone's watch, but they did not find the one Olga wore. She had it on her ankle, hidden underneath her bobby sock. She had told Gretel she did not intend to remove it from there until they reached American-occupied soil. Fortunately, Gretel had sewn a secret slash pocket in the side seam of her skirt, where Jakob's ring was safe.

Again, the soldiers motioned the Germans to finish the soup, and this time they did just that. One by one, each person gave a nod of gratitude and then moved on.

Not far from Pilsen, they were resting by the road when a shiny military car pulled up. The four Russian officers in it ordered Gretel to come to the car. The armband had once again given her away as being the leader.

"Olga, please. You have my parents' address. Contact them if anything happens to me," she whispered.

First Gretel received a chocolate bar from the men, and then they goaded her into taking a swig from a brandy bottle. They chided her about remembering to be respectful to the Russian army and told her to welcome them to German soil.

What did it matter? she thought. Nothing could embarrass her anymore, and she wanted to see that she had a future. What good would it do to resist them if she ended up dead? For that reason, Gretel greeted them heartily, then thanked them one by one and praised their military success. For this, she received four approving grins, and then they were gone.

The push to Pilsen was a hard one for the children. As they schlepped along, the women's words, "We will be there soon," became an empty refrain, and they pouted, no longer believing them. Gretel and Olga became testy, too. They had not expected to be in charge of so many children, and although they asked people along the way to take on the care of the ten siblings, no one wanted the task.

"Here is the name of their mother…She will come to get them soon…You will have no problem…They are well-behaved children," Gretel insisted, but no one offered.

Gretel and Olga tried to leave them at the Pilsen train station, where surely someone would care for them, but the children followed right on their heels.

"Olga, I cannot take them home with me," Gretel whispered.

"I know. Not me, either. They have been through so much."

"I worry most about little Adam, Olga. He is wheezing and I do not know why. He doesn't have asthma. Perhaps it is allergies, or maybe something psychosomatic."

"All the more reason we need to leave them behind, where they will eventually get medical help," urged Olga. "We have a long trip to Kassel. It is not in their best interest to drag them along."

The Red Cross workers at Pilsen fed them some stew, so for the first time in days, they had full stomachs. The two women and the ten children washed up in the restroom and then traveled on together aboard a packed-to-capacity freight train to Leipzig. The littlest children draped themselves around each other and were soon asleep.

The train reached Leipzig in the middle of the night. The railroad station was a dismal sight. It was, in effect, a giant refugee camp with hundreds of people milling about confused, tired, and hungry. The mammoth building, damaged by bombs, had no glass in its once-magnificent arched walkways.

Olga and Gretel settled the children in the large waiting room. The oldest girl quietly dandled the baby on her knee, but the other children whined that they were hungry again. The women told the children to stay put while they searched for food, but they had already decided: they would not return. They had shuttled the brood for days, and now the youngsters would have to make their way by the good deeds of someone else.

"Gretel, do not look back! You must not cry. If we take them farther away from their mother, she may never find them," Olga said sternly.

Gretel opened her mouth as if to say something, but just sighed.

Olga dragged Gretel's suitcase—which both of them now used—to the ticket window where the women inquired where the next train west was going.

"We are headed to Kassel," Gretel said.

"I am sorry, ladies," the man answered. "There are no trains going anywhere west of Leipzig, at least not in the foreseeable future."

Gretel kept a stiff upper lip, but Olga began to sob. "My God! Gretel! We will have to *walk* to Kassel! Isn't that about three hundred kilometers?"

Gretel pointed to a sign listing the distances to various cities. "It says three hundred and twenty-five kilometers."

The two women were pondering what to do, when they noticed an empty pull cart at the end of the train, like the one they had used in Beroun.

"Grab it!" Gretel said in a loud whisper. Quickly, they threw the suitcase in the cart and took off into the dark streets, laughing.

Still panting, Gretel told Olga, "You know, we lost the kids, gained a cart, and I don't feel the least bit guilty. We can travel faster now and find a place to sleep."

Other than agreeing that it was best to stay the night at a hotel and get a fresh start in the morning, the two had little more conversation.

When morning came, they prepared for a long day and a long walk. After breakfast at a restaurant, they each bought what their rations for the week permitted: one-half loaf of bread, a little margarine, eight potatoes, a small piece of liver sausage, and some matches. They had stolen two spoons at the restaurant, and once their wares were loaded in the wagon, they felt ready to handle the walk to Kassel. They knew it could take weeks.

CHAPTER 11

The weather was blustery for the month of May, but Gretel was snug in the warmth of the gray cardigan sweater she had claimed when Gertrude left it hanging on the hook behind the front door of the former schoolteacher's house. Olga had bartered with a hotel employee and traded her watch for a headscarf, a clean gray dress, and a brown wool sweater. The clothes were not new, but she was happy to have them, especially the sweater, since wool was necessary to make uniforms and had been in short supply during wartime. She knew the clothes were most likely stolen goods, swiped from the luggage of a hotel guest, and her watch was not a fair exchange, but she thanked the man abundantly for them.

The two traveled on, walking past the University of Leipzig, a remarkable institution and one of the oldest universities in the world. It stood gallantly against the damage of war with its lofty spires and epochal architecture still intact.

Olga sighed. "I wanted to attend a school like that. If only the war had not changed things."

"I was engaged to a doctor once," Gretel told her. "His name was Wilhelm. He died in an attack on a field hospital before I ever went to Poland. Plans changed for me, too."

Olga took Gretel's hand in hers, looked into her eyes, and said haltingly, "Oh, Gretel, I am so sorry." Gretel pulled her hand away from Olga's and patted her on the shoulder. She did not elaborate further, and Olga did not pursue it.

They strolled on with little conversation for another twenty minutes. Gretel was deep in thought, musing over Wilhelm and Jakob, as they walked past a hospital. Before she had time to react, a Russian guard had grabbed her by the arm and without a word began ushering her up the cold stone steps of the hospital.

Olga looked puzzled but kept mum. Gretel dared not question the soldier, either, and went along obediently. Olga did not try to tag along. Instead, she stayed outside and watched over the coveted handcart.

Once inside, the soldier led Gretel to the hospital's reception desk, where the receptionist asked to see her travel papers. "So, you have some medical training. That's good. We need you here," she said. Gretel realized her Red Cross band had given her away—again! She made herself a mental promise to toss the band and her medicine bag at the next feasible moment.

"I have to speak to my companion, if I may," Gretel said nervously. The receptionist translated what she said to the Russian guard who had commandeered Gretel's help. The guard allowed her to speak to Olga, and even though he did not speak German, he stood within listening distance.

"They say they need me, Olga, but I do not know why. Take the cart, go back to the hotel, and stay the night. I will find you in the morning."

An impatient sigh from the guard caused Gretel to flinch nervously, and she followed him back to the reception desk without a chance to elaborate with Olga about their plans.

A nurse came from nowhere, leaned over the receptionist's shoulder, and copied down Gretel's information. Then she wrote something else on a separate piece of paper and handed it to Gretel, who noticed the handwriting first, before she ever read

what it said. The penmanship was perfect, a form of artistic cal-
ligraphy so lovely it took Gretel aback. Once she focused on what
it said, Gretel saw that among the words indicating the date and
time and the nurse's signature was the term *"Freiwilliger."* Gretel
put her hand over her mouth and silently mouthed into it, "I am
not a volunteer!"

"Go to the second floor," instructed the nurse. "At the top of
the stairs there will be a desk. Give the woman there the paper I
just gave you, sign in, and they will show you what to do." She put
her hand gently on Gretel's forearm and wished her good luck,
but in words that held a frightening undertone, she admonished,
"This place is guarded, so mind what you do."

Gretel signed in, and the head nurse there, a tall young
woman with sable eyes who introduced herself as Agnes, showed
Gretel a small kitchen where she could get a little something to
eat. Agnes left, but just as Gretel finished some bread and tea,
she reappeared. She led Gretel to a clinical-looking dorm-like
room. "This is where you will sleep," she said matter-of-factly and
then showed Gretel where she could take a bath.

Agnes also gave her a crisp, clean nursing assistant's uniform
to wear. It was a light-blue pinafore over a white blouse with an
insignia patch and a dark-blue skirt. This didn't seem too terrible a situation, Gretel surmised, so she bathed and dressed as
directed, vowing to wash her hair and do something about the
itching on her head before she left, which would be soon, she figured, since she did not intend to stay the night.

She had just finished dressing when, as if on cue, Agnes
returned. Agnes seemed to know her every move, and so Gretel
began to suspect there were spies about. "You will be working in
the women's unit," Agnes said, indicating Gretel should follow
her. Short Gretel stepped lively to keep up with the long-legged
woman as they went through a series of hallways and double
doors that led to the south wing.

It was there that Gretel first realized the reason they had sum-
moned her for help. There were dozens of anguished-looking
women, old ladies, and young girls. Some were on beds in the
hallway, some in wards. Among their injuries was an array of knife

wounds, split lips, scratches, and bruises. They all seemed in shock. Many of them were silent, staring straight ahead, but others were whimpering or babbling.

Gretel's disbelieving and puzzled facial expression drew a response. "*Sie wurden geraubt,*" Agnes said.

"Raped? All of them?" Gretel gasped.

With her lower lip quivering, Agnes answered, "*Ja. Die rote Armee.*"

Gretel could not believe Red Army soldiers would rape children, too. "*Was? Die Kinder?*" she asked.

Agnes sighed softly. "*Ja. Kinder auch,*" she said as she patted the hand of an eleven-year-old girl and then checked the damage to the child's raw vaginal lips.

Gretel was aghast that such things would continue when the war was supposedly over and the once-great demagogue that was Hitler was dead. Agnes went on to explain that the Red Army leaders had promised the soldiers they could "take" any German woman they wanted without consequence if they helped win the war, and some men staked their claim on that promise.

"Report the dying immediately," Agnes instructed. "Other than that, you need to treat their wounds, listen to their stories, or hold their hand if they want you to. It is all we can do. There are a few new victims each day, so be prepared for that."

Despite the carnage and violence she had already experienced, Gretel's mind catapulted into a zone of disbelief she had never reached before. No doubt those who would do such a thing were the most foul, decayed offal of the human race. But there was work to do, so she tried not to dwell on it.

A woman's sobbing drew Gretel's attention toward a bed with two people in it. She stared gape-mouthed at a woman who shared a bed with her eight-year-old daughter. Both had been severely beaten and brutally raped. "How can I face her father when he gets home?" the woman said.

All Gretel could think to say was, "It's not your fault."

A Red Guard walked past, blathering something in Russian that Gretel could not totally understand, but the gist of it was: she had best get busy.

Some of the victims had been gang-raped for hours! Two women were literally hemorrhaging to death, but there was not enough blood for transfusions to save them. Gretel tried to get as much information about the patients' names and addresses as possible, under the guise that it was for bookkeeping purposes. The sad truth was that the information would be useful for identification when notifying family members of their deaths.

The oldest victim, who was seventy years old, pleaded, "*Beten Sie mit mir,*" but Gretel could not get herself to pray with her. Instead, she gently stroked the frail, elderly woman's silver hair for a time, and then left to tell Agnes about the prayer request.

"Is there a minister here?" Gretel asked. "That woman wants someone to pray with her, and I will not be a hypocrite."

Gretel did not need to explain to Agnes why she could not pray. Instead, Agnes nodded and left to find the one member of the clergy who was there.

Gretel's shift ended at 2000 hours. She had done all she could, so she changed out of the uniform and tried to leave. A Russian guard, a more handsome but grimier-looking man than the one she had first met, stopped her at the door. He asked in German if she lived in Leipzig. Gretel was grateful he knew German and began to explain. "*Ich bin von Kassel. Ich muss gehen.*"

"*Nein!*" he said emphatically and told her she could not leave for Kassel, because they only granted passes to those who lived within Leipzig city proper. In desperation, she tried to enlighten him about Olga, but he just smirked. When he picked his nose and deposited his find on his sleeve, Gretel turned away in disgust. Outwardly, she appeared calm, but inwardly, she began to panic.

Although she had already eaten dinner, Gretel went to the little kitchen again; she was not ready to go to bed in the uneasy confines of the dorm room. A friendly looking German intern who introduced himself as Alfonse pulled up a chair beside Gretel. After the initial polite chitchat, she began to confide in him and told him of her plight. She and many others had lived so vicariously in the shadow of Hitler's regime that forbidding her and those like her to go home seemed vindictive, they agreed.

"The Allies won! What more do they want?" Alfonse said a little too loudly.

Gretel answered in a whisper, "The German people have suffered so much in support of our homeland. Most of us are honorable citizens, not warmongers, but we are all treated the same—like criminals!"

"I know," Alfonse said, speaking more softly now.

Gretel was near tears. "I was a kindergarten teacher. I had a job to do and I did it admirably, but that is over. Why won't they just let me go home, Wilhelm?"

Her slip of the tongue drew a questioning look from Alfonse. The hospital setting, the doctor's uniform he wore, and even his particular regional dialect reminded her so much of Wilhelm, her very first love, but Gretel did not explain to Alfonse why she misspoke. Instead, she bid him a good night and went to bed.

The next morning Alfonse and Gretel met again at breakfast.

"I have thought up a plan for your escape," he told her. "I will explain it to you, but do not do anything just yet."

Gretel followed him to a storage room, where he showed her a linen closet. "Meet me here at twenty hundred hours when I go off duty, and I will try to help you escape," he said. "Until then, make sure no one is watching and hide your things under the blankets in here. Do not try to leave until I make sure the way is clear."

At lunchtime, Gretel slipped away from the ward to hide her purse and coat under the stacks of bedding in the closet, as Alfonse had instructed. When she was done, she turned around to see a nurse she had met earlier in the day entering the room. Because the nurse had an abrasive personality that she did not trust, Gretel was thankful when the woman did not appear to suspect that Gretel was doing anything other than checking inventory. There were spies who would gladly report to the guards that Gretel was planning to run away—in exchange for favors, that is—but the consequences for Gretel would be severe.

At precisely the arranged time, Gretel entered the storeroom. An orderly was there, so Gretel pretended to be busy by fumbling with some syringes. When he left, Gretel began to breathe heavily in anticipation of her escape. Her throat felt parched, and her heart raced as she waited for Alfonse. Would he come? If she did get away, would Olga even be at the hotel? After all, they had agreed to meet in the morning, and it was now nightfall!

When Alfonse came, he took action immediately. With hardly a word, he grabbed several sheets and tied the first to a metal radiator. He knotted a second sheet, tied it to the first, and then added a third one and a fourth. He stuck the improvised rope out the open window and helped Gretel on with her coat. To Gretel's surprise, Alfonse pulled her close and kissed her on the forehead. As he cupped his hands to boost her to the window frame, he said, "*Auf Wiedersehen, kleine Dame!*"

The "little lady," as he called Gretel, was in such a state of terror and shock she forgot to say good-bye in return.

Since she was only on the second floor, it was not difficult for Gretel to drop her purse to the ground, along with a bundle she had tied up containing the clothes she wore there. Then she climbed down the knotted sheet rope while Alfonse steadied it. She lost a shoe as she landed, and when she bent over to put it on, she noticed the distinct smell of vomit in the alley. There was most likely a drunken soldier nearby, and the thought terrified her so much that Gretel ran full speed through the dark streets to the hotel, arriving just minutes before the 2100 hours military-imposed curfew.

Assuming Olga was in the same room they had earlier occupied, Gretel darted through the hotel lobby to the door that indicated room 14. There, as Gretel and Olga had planned, she rapped three times slow, three times fast, then twice. Olga opened the door, and the two embraced, this time not awkwardly, as new acquaintances might do, but as the dearest of friends.

Gretel noticed that one of Olga's front teeth was missing. It had wiggled some ever since she endured the beating at the Czech/German border, but over time it had become very loose and now was gone entirely. Gretel felt sorry for her, because

Olga's short, crudely chopped hair and missing tooth made her look a little clownish, but Gretel had become fond of this woman, who had been through so much and yet managed to smile a somewhat toothless smile.

The women chatted nonstop while Gretel changed out of the nursing assistant's uniform. "I am anxious to get going first thing in the morning," Gretel told Olga. "I cannot wait until my parents meet you. My mother can be a little standoffish, but you will adore my father. He has such a great sense of humor! I need to get word to them that I am on my way home."

Gretel, with Olga in tow, asked at the hotel desk how she might send a telegram. "I want to send my parents a message that I am on the way home," she said with clear delight in her voice.

The clerk lit a cigarette, took a long drag, and with it still hanging from his lips, he began to chastise her. "Lady, there are no phones, no telegraphs, no mail, and no newspapers or radio. Do not even think about a bus or train! There is no communication! Such things were government controlled and financed, and now the government no longer exists! Now, stop bothering me!"

Despite the peevishness of this man—the same one who had bartered with Olga regarding the clothes—Gretel and Olga were polite to him. After all, they agreed, he was a victim of war, too.

Even if they had wanted to, the two women dared not leave until curfew ended at 0600 hours, so after Gretel ditched the nursing uniform and Red Cross band in the first-floor communal bathroom, they turned in. The room had one bed with an old smelly mattress, but Gretel slept a deep sleep that night, curled up against Olga. This time, without dreaming of Jakob.

The next morning Gretel dressed and put on Jakob's ring, which she had hidden for weeks in the slash pocket of her skirt. She sighed for the days of their passionate lovemaking and their exhilarating clandestine affair, but there were no more tears left to cry. Perhaps he had mailed a letter to her mother, perhaps not; even so, it wouldn't have reached her. It was time to go home to Kassel.

The Red Cross was serving oatmeal in the hotel lobby, so the women ate their fill in preparation for their long journey to

Kassel. Neither Olga's dowdy clothing, nor the sight of her hair standing askew embarrassed Gretel. She saw only the beauty of her companion's patient soul.

"A third helping of oatmeal?" Olga teased, rubbing her tongue against the bare spot where her tooth was missing. "If you weren't so skinny, Gretel, and if we didn't need the calories for our walk, I would get after you!" She giggled.

"*Ja, mein Freund,*" Gretel laughed, then mimicked the face of a chipmunk with full cheeks.

Gretel put on her coat, and it was only then that she found a piece of paper in one of the pockets. Immediately, she recognized the beautiful handwriting as belonging to the first nurse she had met at the Leipzig hospital. It read simply, "Good luck to you!" It reminded her of the day Lieutenant Hinkley had put a piece of strudel in that very same coat pocket before she left the jail in Posen. Her incarceration, that enormous and pivotal event in her life, now seemed so long ago, but these small kindnesses amid the horrors of war would give her strength to trudge on to Kassel.

By late afternoon, the trekkers had traveled about fourteen kilometers. Each time they went uphill, they pulled the cart; when going downhill, they sat on it, with the rear person using her shoes for brakes, while the one in the front guided the tongue between her feet. It was a tricky maneuver, but it gave them a chance to act silly, like schoolchildren on a playground, and it felt so good to laugh.

Occasionally they would go into a ditch, tip over, or both. Eventually, Olga wore the soles of her shoes paper thin and it did not seem like a game anymore. Gretel promised her a new pair when they got to Kassel.

As night moved in, they searched for a place to stay. Throughout their gnarly adventure, nighttimes were always the scariest. Olga began biting her nails, and as the daylight waned, she wearily plunked herself on the ground. With pursed lips she said, "You are pushing me beyond my limits, Gretel Sennhenn! We have to find some shelter for the night. Otherwise, well, you just keep going! Walk to Kassel! Go then! I refuse!"

Gretel stood with her hands on her hips, "I do not have the strength to continually prod you and motivate you the way we did with the children! Get up off the ground!"

"Don't get testy with me! I do not have the gumption to go on!"

"Please, Olga. I am dirty, tired, and I want to find a place to sleep, too," Gretel said. Then, with a half smile, she added, "Anyway, I'm afraid to go on without you."

Olga stood up, and wiped off the remains of a sniffle with the back of her hand. Gretel rubbed a tear off Olga's cheek with her thumb, and they kept on walking for another fifteen minutes. Though neither held a grudge from their short spat, they didn't speak to one another until they smelled smoke.

Olga cried out, "*Was das IST?*"

Gretel flattened her hand against Olga's mouth to quiet her and said as softly as she could, "*Es ist die rote Armee.*"

From their distance, they noticed a number of Russian tanks blocking the highway and hundreds of people milling about or sitting around campfires. Through the darkled, smoky haze, they watched one of the tanks pull forward, after which the soldiers allowed about fifty of the Germans to pass through the blockade and scramble to the American-controlled side. Then the tank pulled back, and a new group moved up to await their turn. The soldiers had no reason to delay these people, other than to annoy and humiliate them. Children cried. Adults talked in low tones. Obviously, they were restless and scared, but to make things worse, it started to rain.

Gretel and Olga realized their best course of action now was to stay quiet and unnoticed, so their only communication was through gestures. In an effort to become less visible, Gretel buttoned her cardigan sweater to cover the white blouse underneath it.

With both of them grasping the handle of the cart, lest they separate, they made their way unseen to a small wooded area. Their intention was to return to a village they had passed a short distance away, but soon they spotted another blockade.

Reluctantly, they drew deeper into the woods to look for a place to bed down for the night.

That's when they heard someone singing in German. It was a man's voice belting out the words to a marching song, "*Lore, Lore, Lore!*" The voice belonged to a lone, hoary-headed, elfin-looking elderly man who was leaning against a tree.

He was visually perusing the silhouette of Olga's ample breasts when he asked, "Do you have any food or money? This is the border between the Russian- and American-controlled land. I can show you how to cross over it."

He did not look as if he had come far, because he appeared neither malnourished nor dirty. The strange man mumbled something that was incomprehensible and repeated to Gretel and Olga that here was the boundary between the Russian and American zones. There was a way around the tanks, he explained, and it was rough, but not impossible.

They gave him four potatoes, their piece of liver sausage, and a nice sum of money. He thanked them politely, and they followed him through the woods. They had to stop often, lifting the cart over bumps and bramble and pulling it out of holes. He did not help, but slowly walked on mumbling continuously such things as, "My poor Germany! They must let me open the school! Where is our strong army? We have to win, or they will butcher us all!"

He sat down suddenly, sobbing, but after a moment of reflection, he stood up and moved very close to Gretel. His action did not startle her, since his demeanor seemed neither annoying nor frightening. Most likely he was trying to see her more clearly in the darkness, Gretel assumed. He stared her square in the eyes, his nose very close to her own. Gretel did not flinch, but Olga backed up a few steps.

"Now you are in America. I have to go back to the red devils. The children are always hungry! Cross the field ahead and you can see the road."

He began laughing as if this was all a big joke, shouted, "*Auf Wiedersehen!*" and turned back into the woods. Had this odd man, who was flouncing around the woods on a rainy night, simply gammoned them to get their supplies?

After another hour of pushing on, tugging and pulling on the cart, the women reached the edge of a highway and sat down. It had taken all their strength to get there, trudging across a freshly plowed and muddy field; and now, despite the rain, they sat devouring slices of bread with margarine on it, while mired in mindless chatter and nervous laughter.

So caught up were they in just surviving another night, they did not notice they were less than ten meters from a cabin; but when the rain began to pour harder and the wind picked up, their attention was drawn to the sound of a tree branch slapping its roof.

Gretel motioned for Olga to stay put while she crawled across the muddy ground to its front entrance. As she stood to try the front door, a rotten porch board creaked, and she dropped to her knees again.

Gretel felt a hand clutch her right leg just above the top of her sock. With no attempt to minimize the shriek in her voice, she shouted, *"Nicht Olga! Bleiben Sie weg!"*

Olga backed off in a hurry. "I didn't mean to frighten you," she whispered.

"Go back! Stay with the cart!"

Gretel tried the entrance, and finding it locked, walked quietly and stealthily to the back door, though there was no need for the silence, since no one could have heard her over the sounds of the rainstorm.

In the back of the building was another door, and it was wide open. By the light of her matches, Gretel tapped her way around inside and discovered two rooms, one quite large, the second a small storage space. To shed more light on the situation, she lit the wood-burning stove with a few sticks of wood that were next to it. It was too good to believe! There were two bunk beds and a stack of blankets. It was all they needed for the night, except water.

"Olga! Come quickly!" Gretel yelled.

Olga came at a dead run, and the two hugged and leapt for joy! "We are going to make it now, I know we will!" Olga said. Normally stoic Gretel lost her composure and sobbed.

After they put a dish outside to catch rainwater, they went to bed. It was midmorning when a sunbeam taunted Olga and woke her from her deep sleep.

"*Gretel! Wachen Sie auf!*" she squealed.

Gretel woke then, too, and began to totter around in a sleepy haze to see what it was that had Olga so excited.

There, in the storeroom, was a big sack of powdered milk, a bag of oatmeal, dried soup powder, a few cook pots, silverware, a box of laundry soap, and all sorts of medical supplies.

Gretel spied a bottle of Kuprex and gasped. Kuprex was a head lice treatment! Is that why her head had been itching for days?

The women checked each other's heads, and it was true: they both had head lice. They spent the day treating their hair, washing clothes in the rain barrel, and drying them by the fire. After a good night's rest, they would set out in the morning. This time, in the American-controlled zone.

After much discussion, the women decided the army must have commandeered the cabin and used it as a field hospital. They could see that the soil had been disturbed as if tents had once been set up there, and the medical supplies were an obvious clue. No matter what its use, or who owned it, the cabin was a wonderful find, and the powdered soup and oatmeal would be enough to keep them alive for the rest of the lengthy walk to Kassel.

Although they left shortly after sunrise the next morning, the first time Gretel and Olga met up with any members of the American occupation was in the early afternoon. They were now about a hundred and fifty kilometers and days away from Leipzig. They were so terribly exhausted that Gretel barely flinched when a dark-skinned American soldier stopped them as they walked along the highway.

He wanted to see their passes for the American Zone. He said they would have to go back to Leipzig to get them.

"We have come so far and mean no harm, sir. We just want to move on to Kassel, please," Olga said in her meager but understandable English.

Gretel feigned an emotional collapse and managed to cry tears, which she wiped with the palm of her hand. The sunlight glistened on the engagement ring Jakob had given her.

The soldier demanded the ring in exchange for their passing. She had heard the American soldiers were not such thieves as the Russians, but clearly what she had heard was wrong. Now there was no one left to trust!

The soldier tried to take the ring off of her hand, but she pushed his hand away, took it off herself, and gave it to him without reluctance or sadness. Perhaps it was the only way to end World War II as she knew it and lived it. Gretel was not a male, not a soldier from any country, and she was not a Jew. She was a German citizen, a female, who saw the war from a different vantage point. Perhaps now that she had given up her last possession of value, the war would be over for her.

On May 31, 1945, nearly a month after leaving Poland, Gretel and Olga reached Kassel on foot. Olga rested for two weeks and then traveled to her hometown. But for Gretel, the city of Kassel was just one more sojourn along life's journey, and eventually she would continue her travels to the west.

EPILOGUE

In Kassel, Gretel found her mother, who was happy to see her, but too absorbed in her own woes and her own sorrow to listen to Gretel's story. Gretel's father had been killed; they had never heard from her brother, but it was rumored that he was part of a Nazi breeding program in Norway, one intended to produce the "ideal" Aryan race Hitler so admired.

After having lived the life of a wealthy person, her mother now existed in the two rooms she shared with another woman and their most meager of belongings.

Gretel took a small room above a pub and worked part-time jobs to help support her mother and set aside a savings for her in her old age.

In early 1946 Gretel met a Norwegian-born American soldier stationed there, who would become the man she would marry. His name was Olaf. "My Ole," she called him. He was a kind, gentle man, a farmer from Wisconsin. In early 1947 they had a son, whom they named Sven. Late that November, upon Olaf's release from the Army, the family flew to New York to begin their life in the United States.

When they arrived in New York, the streets were brilliant with Christmas decorations, and the hustle and bustle of shoppers awed Gretel, for only hours earlier, she had left Germany with its near-empty stores and devastated buildings; now, here in America, she was in what appeared to be a fairyland.

She held her little boy, showed him the Statue of Liberty, and said, "Look, son. This is America! It will be our home now!" Two days later at Central Station, they boarded a train to Wisconsin, where she eased into the life of a farm wife.

Occasionally Gretel would think of Jakob, especially when she was in the barn, but the war was over, and so was her life in Europe.

One day when Sven was just four, he wanted her to play "hide and seek."

"Mamma, *Ich finde Sie!*" he said.

Those had been Jakob's last words to her, and they might have pained her, but instead she smiled and said, "No, son. You must say things in English now. Say, 'I will find you.'"

Gretel lived a contented life on the farm, and although she missed her mother, she never returned to Germany and never regretted it. She said the train the little family had taken from New York to Wisconsin would be her last train west, and so it was.